MURDER AT ST. MARK'S

Dr. Wignall, Headmaster of the venerable public school of St. Mark's, is fiercely proud of the institution. But this pride has been considerably shaken by the murder of a teacher's daughter in the nearby woods. As Mr. Prenderby, the charismatic master of North House, uncovers a sordid undercurrent of gambling, blackmail and immorality amongst the school-boys, another murder is committed — this time, one of the pupils. When one of the teachers bolts, the police think they are trailing the killer — but are they?

D1428485

NORMAN FIRTH

MURDER AT ST. MARK'S

Complete and Unabridged

LINFORD
Leicester

First published in Great Britain

First Linford Edition
published 2015

A catalogue record for this book is available
from the British Library.

ISBN 978–1–4448–2555–8

Published by
F. A. Thorpe (Publishing)
Anstey, Leicestershire

Set by Words & Graphics Ltd.
Anstey, Leicestershire
Printed and bound in Great Britain by
T. J. International Ltd., Padstow, Cornwall

This book is printed on acid-free paper

Author's Foreword:

Before you begin to read this novel, I feel I must make it clear that the views held, and the opinions expressed herein, by various of the characters, are not to be taken as my own.

The St. Mark's public school of the story is entirely imaginary, as are the characters in the story.

If this work may seem to dwell upon the sordid and seamy side of the life of the boys, I would like you to allow me your indulgence, and not to assume that the incidents mentioned are there for anything but the atmosphere of the story, which does not set out to be a true portrayal of public school life, but merely to entertain, and, perhaps, horrify. The public school system of England has turned out some wonderful sportsmen and leaders — plus a code for its students. But there are black sheep in every flock, and if St. Mark's seems to bear more than its share of those sheep, remember, please, that this is, after all, just a 'story'!

Norman Firth,
Birkenhead,
July 1949.

1

Mr. Prenderby is Bored

There were subdued coughs from various parts of the Hall, a scraping of chairs as boys and parents settled themselves more comfortably, then a silence again as Dr. Samuel Walter Wignall rose and moved forward to the Speaker's table.

Placing his fingertips upon the green baize he paused to allow a moment for last-minute disturbances; then, clearing his throat portentously, he spoke.

'Ladies and gentlemen,' he said, with an embracing glance at the ranks of faces before him. 'Ladies and gentlemen — boys — and you inky little rascals in the junior forms — '

Here he paused again, to direct a paternal smile upon the inky little rascals, who preserved an outraged and dignified silence. The paternal smile was followed by a smile directed at the parents — a broad smile this time, to show how human he was, despite his responsibilities as Headmaster and controlling spirit of a school as famous as St. Mark's.

Mr. Prenderby, the master of North House, sat back in his chair with an audible sigh. He had listened to Dr. Wignall's peculiarly toneless voice each Speech Day for eight years. He knew exactly what was coming. It never varied. Prenderby was supremely bored.

Wignall said: 'I have always appreciated the privilege of being able to say a few words to you all at end of term; it is pleasant to gaze back upon the school's attainments and to summarise the sporting and educational activities of the boys. It is not my intention to detain you overlong — '

'Nevertheless, I bet he talks for at least half an hour,' said Mr. Prenderby in a daring whisper to Mr. Brooks, who sat beside him. 'He always does — '

Brooks, who was pretty raw, having come down from Oxford only that term, grinned as Prenderby went on:

'Now he'll say: 'First let us take the

field of physical endeavour' — '

'First,' said Dr. Wignall, moving aside a water glass, and gazing at the baize cloth as if it were a football pitch, 'let us take the field of physical endeavour — '

They took the field of physical endeavour, and learned that the St. Mark's Junior Cricket Eleven had soared away to a fine start, and played good, consistent cricket throughout the season. They were, doubtless, cheered and encouraged by the news that the St. Mark's First Football Eleven bade fair to be in a prominent position in the Junior League when the season closed. They were informed that Mills Major had carried off with ease the Dunderfield Gold Trophy for swimming.

Having passed over the world of sport, Wignall continued:

'And, leaving the realms of athletic prowess, let us review briefly the more *important* side of school affairs; namely, the scholastic record for the past year . . . '

Busy with thoughts of the Highland holiday on which he proposed to embark,

Mr. Prenderby heard only dimly how Bagshott Minimus had displayed marked genius in the Founder's Junior Scholarship Award Examinations; how Jones of the Sixth had captured the Tullen Literary Award; and how Grass of the Fourth had walked away with the silver medal for the Goldman English History, Sitting and Oral.

' . . . and so we may look back upon the last few months as having more than upheld the prestige of St. Mark's, both on playing field and in classroom — ' said Dr. Wignal; Prenderby sat up again, and murmured to Brooks:

'He's drawing near the end now. Now comes: 'It is an honour, and one which I feel keenly, to be Headmaster of this ancient establishment' — '

Dr. Wignall turned and frowned momentarily, as the muttering voice disturbed his poise. Then returning to his audience he went on: 'It is an honour, and one which I feel *deeply* . . . '

'Damn!' said Prenderby in an annoyed whisper. 'He's said *keenly* every other year — '

' . . . to be Headmaster of this ancient establishment.'

Prenderby muttered: 'When next we meet there will be many new faces — '

'When next we meet there will be many new faces,' said Dr. Wignall.

'And many now present will be absent . . . ' Prenderby whispered.

'And many now present will be absent,' boomed Wignall, in a gentler tone of voice. 'But wherever they may go in life, whatever the world may have in store for them, I feel confident they will never forget St. Mark's, and the green playing fields, the grey old stones, the river, and the woo — -'

Dr. Wignall pulled himself up sharply. There was a fragmentary pause, which gave Prenderby an opportunity to murmur in Brooks' ear: 'He almost put his foot in it that time, old man. He was going to say 'and the *woods*', and just stopped himself in time.'

'Why?' whispered back Brooks, curiously.

'The murder, man,' said Prenderby. 'You heard about it, didn't you?'

'Oh, of course. It wouldn't do to bring it up before the parents, I don't suppose.'

Dr. Wignall, recovering neatly from his blunder, was continuing. 'I hope and believe that the new pupils who will be joining us next term will carry forward the good name of St. Mark's, and uphold the strong pride which has always been our tradition — that they too will grow to know and love every inch of the school, as their predecessors have . . . '

'And that when they go out into the wide world, as many of you are doing today, they will go well-equipped and armed for the stern battle which lies before us all,' supplied Mr. Prenderby, ironically.

'And that when, they go out into the wide world, as many of you are doing today, they will go well-equipped and armed for the stern battle which lies before us all,' said Dr. Wignall, a triumphant note sounding in his voice, now.

'There remains only one item,' whispered Prenderby.

'There remains only one item,' said Dr. Wignall, unconscious of the smile on

Brooks' features behind him. 'That is, to name our top house for this term — the honour, both on the field and in the classroom, has been won, and justly, by North House, under the able guidance of Mr. Prenderby!'

There was a burst of applause and some cheering from the noisier fags, all of which was accepted by Dr. Wignall with a smile and a nod, and Mr. Prenderby with yawning hugely.

'Good luck to you all,' Dr. Wignall said, taking one pace back from the table. 'And when we meet next term, let us meet with the determination that once again we will give of our best to St. Mark's!'

And with a smile and a nod he stepped backwards, trod on Prenderby's sprawled feet, staggered, muttered something, made a rather startling recovery considering his sixty-three years, and sat down in his chair.

★   ★   ★

'Funny,' said Prenderby, later, in his study.

'What's funny?' queried Brooks, looking up from a timetable.

'Old Wignall . . . he usually cracks that old chestnut about education being a drawing-out and not a putting-in — he missed it this year. Of course, the slip he made when he mentioned the woods may have flustered him.'

Brooks frowned: 'Really, Prenderby,' he said slowly, 'I can't quite see what that murder has to do with the school. I mean, after all, murders *happen* — don't they? I mean, they happen all over the place, and — '

'True,' agreed Prenderby, carefully packing his rack of pipes in an open suitcase. 'But although the world is chock-full of corpses, Dr. Wignall strongly objects to having any of them anywhere near St. Mark's. What makes it even worse is that it happened to be the daughter of one of our masters — poor Gregg. It was a damn nasty shock for him, I know. And so near the school — '

Brooks murmured: 'I'm afraid I was pretty raw here then, I didn't really *know* Gregg's daughter at the time — but from what I did see of her, she was a — a — '

'Smasher?' suggested Prenderby with a smile.

Brooks grinned. 'I do fall down rather badly on my adjectives,' he admitted.

' 'Smasher' describes her quite as well as anything,' said Prenderby. 'She was an exceedingly quiet and pretty girl, but not without a certain amount of life beneath her reserved ways.'

'How did she happen to be in the woods so late at night?'

Prenderby frowned. 'She was walking home. She'd been here to see her father — as you know, her mother is dead, and she was brought up by a couple in the village. Gregg felt rather ill that night, and sent Paget of the Sixth to see her home. Paget twisted his ankle, and had to be helped back to the school. She left him here, and instead of bothering another escort, started walking herself . . . then . . . '

'I know the rest,' muttered Brooks, with a shudder, 'Her naked and mutilated body was found the following day near the centre of the woods. She'd been horribly assaulted and then murdered. Ugh!'

Prenderby nodded. 'I've always fancied myself as a bit of a detective,' he confessed, ruefully, 'but I'm blessed if I could find anything out about *that* affair. And I went into it quite thoroughly.'

Brooks closed the timetable. 'It had the police more than baffled too, didn't it?'

'It did. Gregg himself was determined to know who'd done it; you remember how he used to wander about like the ghost of Hamlet's father? If you ask me, it was wise of Old Wignall to send him away for the rest of term. Let's hope his mind's easier when he returns next term.'

'Then he *is* coming back next term?' asked Brooks.

'That's the understanding.'

Brooks laid down the timetable and lit a cigarette. He said thoughtfully: 'Don't most schools allow the wives of the masters to live on the premises?'

'I wouldn't say *most* schools,' said Prenderby. 'Some do. As a matter of fact, when I first arrived here, St. Mark's was operating such an arrangement.'

'Then how did the ruling that masters were to accommodate their wives and families elsewhere come about?'

Prenderby laughed. 'That was quite a scandal. Wignall, with the aid of the Board of Governors, made that ruling. You see, we had a rather old-fashioned French Master here. Although he was about fifty himself, he was married to the most charming piece of Parisienne frippery I've seen in many a day. It so happened that one night, whilst Monsieur Gascon was in the Masters' Common Room, the Headmaster went along to his private rooms thinking he would find him there.

'He didn't. He found his wife there — if I remember rightly, her name was Susette — and with the wife, he found *Hawkins of the Sixth*. They weren't playing Ludo, either.

'Of course, Hawkins got the sack, but most of us thought he was a lucky devil anyway, and that Susette's favours were cheap at the price. I always had said myself that Hawkins would go far in his time — I haven't had the chance of seeing

11

him since he left here, but I understand he has had five paternity suits filed against him, and that he was named as co-respondent in three divorce cases. So I consider my opinion was upheld.

'Monsieur Gascon and his wife left the school soon after that incident; and the ruling that wives and daughters must be kept *off the premises* was brought in.'

Brooks whistled, looking at Prenderby. Then said: 'I say — it's just struck me — *you* aren't married, are you, old man?'

Prenderby smiled. 'Only fools and poor men get married, Brooks,' he said. 'And I'm neither.'

* * *

Of those seniors from Prenderby's house who were leaving that term, Raynor was the last to see him. They shook hands.

'So you're leaving us, Raynor?' Prenderby said, conventionally.

'Yes sir,' said Raynor, with rather too much eagerness.

'You have some future in view?'

'Oh, yes sir. I'm going out to India. The

pater's got a shipping business out there.'

Prenderby said: 'How many times, Raymond, have I told you the word is *father*, and not 'pater'? You don't want people to think you're affected, do you?'

'No, sir.'

'Then the word is *father*. Remember that. And if you ever happen to be in the district, I'll be glad to see you again, my boy.'

'Thank you, sir, I'd like to write if I may.'

'By all means do.' They all asked that. All promised to write. Once they were away from St. Mark's, though, they all seemed to forget. Mr. Prenderby's young but compelling personality became little more than an insubstantial past, for which Prenderby was duly grateful. He had as little desire to hear from them as they had to write to him.

'Oh, Raynor,' he called, as that young gentleman opened the door to make his hasty exit. 'I'd like you to do one last little thing for me — tell Beasly that I want him in my study, will you? *At once.*'

Raynor nodded, and the door closed

behind him. Mr. Prenderby, cases packed, everything ready for his departure, sat at his desk and reflected that a master's work was never done. After a while he opened the right-hand drawer, and took therefrom a red pocket book of no great dimensions.

This he held in his hand, waiting —

There was a timid tap on the door, and at his invitation to enter, Beasly of the Fourth came in.

Beasly was thin and pale; he possessed lank hair, a long strand of which clung damply to his forehead. His chin was decorated with an assortment of pimples in various stages of eruption, and his nose was long, curved, predatory. His eyes were small and sunken into his skull either side of his nose, and below them were large, dark circles. His neck and his body were thin almost to the point of emaciation. Altogether he was an unsavoury specimen of British boyhood, and one who was no credit to his house either mentally or athletically. He and Prenderby had never got on well together.

Prenderby raised his eyes after a moment and greeted the junior. In quiet but deadly tones, he said: 'Come over here to the desk, Beasly, and explain to me just why you've been gambling lately!'

Beasly started, and a furtive expression chased the blank enquiry from his narrow features.

'I beg your pardon, sir?'

'*Gambling*, Beasly.'

'But *sir* — '

'Don't lie to me,' said Prenderby, sternly. 'It so happens that I have the proof of your activities — is this yours?'

He threw the red pocket book onto the desk, and Beasly jumped, cried: 'Why, where did — '

Then, sullenly: 'Yes.'

Prenderby sighed. He opened the book.

'Beasly, the handwriting in this book matches yours perfectly. I found this book not more than a half-hour ago, in the main corridor. I looked inside to see to whom it belonged. I found a list of racehorses, and the odds and price you wished to lay, beside each. It would seem you have been unwisely keeping a record of your betting transactions for the past few months, Beasly. And according to this book you have gambled *large sums* — and lost very heavily!'

Beasly stammered: 'But I — I — I can *explain* . . . '

'Can you explain how you chanced, to be in possession of enough money to squander almost *four pounds per week* on this pastime?'

Beasly scowled, and Mr. Prenderby's tone became sharper.

'*Can you?*'

Beasly muttered: 'It's *my* business how much money I have,'

'Quite. I have no quarrel with that. But when you choose to *gamble* it away — and when I am perfectly well aware that your guardian allows you only *five pounds a term* for your own pocket, from which you have to pay your Junior Sports Club dues — then, Beasly, I consider I am entitled to know how you chanced to *have* so much money. According to this book, you owe some bookmaker thirty pounds, also. Who, is not stated.'

Beasly was silent. Prenderby placed the

book in his drawer and locked it.

'I understand Dr. Wignall has already left,' he said. 'I am afraid that this little matter must rest now until next term. But you need have no fear that it will be forgotten. You will report to me on the first day of term, in this study. I will then require a full and complete explanation, and we shall see what is to be done in the matter. Now you may go, Beasly.'

Beasly hesitated. Then: 'May I have my book, sir?'

Prenderby grunted: 'You may not!'

Beasly opened his mouth to say something more; then, catching the glint in the eye of his master, thought better of it.

When he had vanished, Prenderby skimmed through the book again, grinned, and muttered: 'Young idiot hasn't even an idea of form! Throwing money away!'

2

Mr. Prenderby Departs

Mr. Prenderby came from the Hall of North House in his coat, hat and gloves, and carrying two cases.

There was a group of juniors standing halfway up the steps, their backs towards him. They were ready to leave, waiting for the return of the school bus to take them stationwards.

Pritchet of the Fourth was talking. Pritchet usually was talking when he wasn't either eating, drinking or sleeping. He was a talkative type.

' . . . so this chap says to the farmer's daughter: 'I hope you're *satisfied*, my dear?', and she answers . . . '

'Hold on — here's Prenny!' hissed one of his companions in a carrying whisper.

Pritchet held on, and innocent faces were turned politely towards Mr. Prenderby. Prenderby halted on the bottom step and looked back.

'Goodbye, boys, and have a pleasant holiday.'

'Thanks, sir. Same to you, sir.'

'And Pritchet — '

'Sir?' said Pritchet blandly.

'If that's the one about the farmer's daughter and the tame bear, it's getting stale, my boy,' said Prenderby amiably.

Then he walked on, leaving Pritchet with a burning face.

He was thoughtful as he made for the waiting taxi. More than ever, he was certain Pritchet was responsible for the outbreak of writing on the lavatory walls that term. Pritchet had a lavatorial mind . . .

Not that Prenderby had any deep personal feelings on the subject of scribbling smutty remarks on privy whitewash. He was given rather to the view that the lavatory was the most likely place for creative thinking — even if that thinking took the form of ill-constructed couplets of an obscene nature. He was still able to smile at one which he had ordered Bronze, the porter, to wash out.

If it was one of Pritchet's, he reflected that Pritchet must be rather clever. It had really been very subtle.

He climbed into the taxi and gave directions. A bunch of seniors at the gates waved to him as he rolled out onto the wide, tree-lined road that led to the station.

His thoughts wandered back to Beasly and his sorry record of losses. He shook his head. Where Beasly could have found so much capital to squander on gambling, he was unable to guess. There had been no reported thefts that term. Nor had any cases of money-lending seen the light of day. Besides, even if Rake of the Fifth was up to his old games, lending any sum from five bob to five quid at twenty percent, would he have lent such amounts to Beasly, a junior, who had no hope of repaying it?

No, Beasly had been up to something. But what?

The gambling was serious enough; there would be a row about that next term when Beasly reported to take his medicine. Dr. Wignall frowned hugely upon that kind of thing. Prenderby himself was inclined to shrug when confronted with misdeeds like gambling, or swearing, or smoking in the top boxroom, and fall back on the old cliché that 'boys would be boys'. In such matters he was an easygoing man. He had once shocked Dr. Wignall by mentioning that it was his opinion the school should be moulded to the boy, and not the boy to the school. A revolutionary thought which had caused Dr. Wignall to regard him with some suspicion for many weeks afterwards.

But Prenderby did his job, and did it well. And whilst he did not wholly approve of severe punishment for what he was pleased to consider 'minor misdeeds', he nevertheless allowed the rules of the school to guide him. His maintenance of discipline in North House was admirable. His boys were, on the whole, the most orderly in the school.

★ ★ ★

Twice each term, the little local station at Munston gave itself up to the encroachment of the pupils of the three nearby schools: St. Mark's, Morefell College and Munston School for Young Ladies.

Twice a term — once when the said pupils were coming, and again when they were going.

The latter was by far the worst of the two: coming, even the rowdier elements were subdued at the thought of yet another school term, with its attendant lessons, impots and lickings before them. Going, a spirit of wild frivolity prevailed, an excess of youthful abandon at the knowledge of the long weeks of freedom ahead. Joy was for the present and unconfined, and recommencement — or, as Mr. Prenderby preferred to call it, 'New Term' — was something far in the hazy future that might never even happen.

At such goings-away as these, the more aged of the four porters lurked in dark corners and wash-houses, leaving the shouting, jostling schoolboys to fend for themselves and carry their own luggage. Schoolboys after a term of penury were not lavish with their tips: a grubby threepenny bit pressed into gnarled hands was small recompense for the wild buffeting to be endured on the outgoing platforms.

A different spirit prevailed on the *return* journey. Laden with treasure-trove scrounged from Maters and Paters, Aunts and Uncles, elder sisters and elder brothers, and such other relations as could be prevailed upon to contribute towards the expenses of a fresh term, the schoolboys were more than generous in their gratuities.

This, however, was end of term, not beginning, and so Mr. Prenderby was compelled, in the absence of porters, to carry his own bags to the local train which would take him to his connection at the nearest big town.

Good-naturedly enough, he shouldered a way through the milling mass on the platform.

Prenderby located a near-empty compartment, and scrambled in. He was viewed without enthusiasm by the three Munston schoolgirls and the four St. Mark's youths, who were already seated, on somewhat intimate terms, therein.

'Room here, I think?' said Mr. Prenderby, and was answered by a restrained 'Yes sir,' from the boys.

He made himself comfortable, and opened his paper. After a few moments a shuffling was audible; and, glancing above the top of the sheet, he perceived the three girls leaving, with meaning glances at their male opposites.

Another minute or two sped into infinity, and then:

'Er — excuse us, sir.'

Prenderby laid the paper aside and glanced at them pleasantly.

'Not going, boys, are you?'

'Well — I think we'll find a place farther back along the — the train. Er — be easier to get to the ticket barrier at the other end.'

Prenderby nodded agreeably. 'Of course. Have a good holiday.'

'Thank you, sir. Same to you, sir.'

They scrambled out hastily, and vanished in the scrum again. Prenderby hoped they'd be able to find their three lady friends. He bore them no malice for their seeming snub; he was under no delusions as to the fascination of the company of a thirty-odd-year-old master, against that of three attractive young girls their own ages. One wasn't able to squeeze the waist of a middle-aged master.

A whistle blew; the engine snorted like an angry dragon. There was a last-minute rush for places, and a great deal of yelling and shouting. A fag was dragged back from sudden death beneath the wheels, and a suitcase burst open, spreading a variety of gymslips, black woollen stockings, underwear, and navy-blue and brown bloomers along the platform. Their owner hastened to retrieve them without a trace of embarrassment.

Prenderby had so far had the luck to keep the carriage to himself; none of the boys were eager to confine themselves in the presence of a master for an hour or two. But at the last minute the door flew open, and someone hurled case and overcoat inside, then tumbled in after them.

'Phew,' said Brooks, thankfully. 'Nearly missed it. I — why, *Prenderby*! I thought you'd gone earlier?'

Prenderby nodded. 'I should have done so. But something cropped up at the last minute. Something always does.'

Brooks fell into the opposite seat and laid his hat beside him. 'I almost missed it myself. Had a thing or two to straighten out.'

Prenderby folded his paper. 'I'm glad you got this train, anyhow. We can have a chat whilst we're on the way. I take it you change at Branshoot?'

'That's right. I'm spending the whole blessed break with an old fossil of an uncle at Brighton. He runs rather to gout and bath-chairs. You know the type. Never knows what the country's coming to, but is quite certain it's the dogs.'

'Why spend the break with him at all?' asked Prenderby.

'Question of diplomacy. The old ass has slightly more than fifteen thousand crisp and crackling quidlets to leave when he finally reaches for his halo. I hope to be on the receiving end of about five thousand of them. I'm his favourite nephew.'

Prenderby grinned, and gazed out of the window. Brooks lit a cigarette and leaned back.

'Hope you enjoy your holiday, old man.'

'I will. I'd enjoy anything that took me away from those little fiends for a while. Be sorry when it's over. The rotten part of it is that I'll have something on my mind the entire break.'

Brooks looked curious, 'School matter?'

'Young Beasly.'

'Oh? What's Beasly been up to?'

'Gambling, apparently. To make it worse, the young idiot was insane enough to keep a written record of his transactions. I happened to find it after he'd dropped it.'

'A written record?'

'In book form. It seems that he's been getting a good deal of money from somewhere, to throw away on horses. Even so, he appears to owe a great deal to some bookmaker.'

'Silly little fool. Did you see him about it?'

'I did. I warned him that he would have

to face the music next term. That was all I could do. I mentioned the large sums he had been losing, in conjunction with his allowance — '

'What did he say?'

'Gave me to understand it was *his* business how much money he had, and not mine.'

'Then you think he has something to hide?'

'I'm pretty sure of it. Or why should he refuse to answer the question? Although the Devil knows how he got his hands on so much. Ran into pounds . . . '

Brooks frowned, 'Personally, I never have liked young Beasly. A pimply little horror! If he's been throwing money away you can be sure he came by it *easily* enough.'

'He'll have plenty of time to think up his defence, anyhow. It'll have to be good, though. Wignall's right down on gambling. He considers it one of the worst forms of malicious mischief the boys could get up to. I shudder to think what he'd say if he knew Baxter of the Sixth takes a book on how long he'll sermonise in Chapel on Sunday mornings. I shudder even more when I think what he'd say if he knew *I* once had ten bob on it, when I was new here, and won three quid.'

Brooks looked at him admiringly 'I expect that's why the boys like you so much — I mean, you're *human*. And I'm not sure it isn't the best way to be. Look where *your* House is. Right on the top of the heap. It's an open secret that when old Wignall retires you'll be offered the Head's House, and all that goes with it. Excluding, of course, the Head's wife.'

'Glad you excluded her,' Prenderby laughed.

'She is rather an old haybag, isn't she?'

'But a haybag who does her part for the welfare of the school very nicely,' Prenderby replied, giving due credit. 'No headmaster could have a wife more suited to the position,'

Brooks grunted. Then: 'I think that if the Head can have a wife on the premises, masters should be allowed the same privilege. I mean, if it's safe enough for the old man's wife, then it's safe enough for, say, mine; if I *had* one. And the reverse applies. If it isn't safe for a master's wife, then it isn't safe for the Head's — is it?'

Prenderby shook his head. 'That argument won't stand up. The Head's a law unto himself; and anyhow, the job really calls for his wife to be on the premises. She has a lot to do with the female staff — matters the Head couldn't handle. Besides — looking at Mrs. Wignall, it's easy to see that if you set her down in the middle of a dormitory and locked her in for the night, she wouldn't be molested. Even if she were younger and better-looking, possessing the personality she now possesses, do you imagine for one moment any junior or senior — or even master — would have the nerve to make any suggestions to her?'

'You're right, of course,' acknowledged Brooks, pulling a face. 'I remember just after I arrived I was guilty of making a remark, which was in slightly dubious taste, in front of her. The frozen stare she gave me would have done credit to a politician who'd been reminded of his pre-election promises.'

Prenderby gave a bored yawn. Both Dr. Wignall and his good lady bored Prenderby frantically.

'Let's talk about something else,' he suggested.

Brook was agreeable. 'We were talking about you being offered the Headmastership. From what I hear myself, it's already a foregone conclusion, that you're 'It' when the Head goes.'

Prenderby looked into space, and was amused at something he saw there. He said, quietly: 'I've been given to understand the same thing by Wignall himself. It appears that I have his personal approval, and that he'd recommended me to the Governors. He told me that at first he'd considered I was a rather *strange* master. My views, he let me know, didn't exactly coincide with his own. He said he was glad to see I'd settled down so nicely, and he felt that when the time came, if I secured the post, I'd carry on where *he'd* left off. In the same old tradition-bound way, he meant, though he put it differently.' Prenderby grinned at Brooks.

'I'm afraid he underestimates me,' he concluded.

'You'd make changes?'

'I couldn't resist the temptation. Of course, once I really got started, I'm very much afraid I wouldn't know where to stop. I'd be carried away by my enthusiasms. I've always believed in a 'free' school. If I had one of my own, I could run it as I wished. But you can't muck about with a commercial proposition, Brooks, old man. And St. Mark's is just that. Once my ideas began to drift through to the world at large, boys would be moved so fast their passing would agitate the air for miles around. It's a most regrettable fact that parents wouldn't stand for the school I'd advocate. They wouldn't wish their precious kids to grow up free of inhibitions and repressions. They like to think the dear little numbskulls are looked after and guarded and guided at every turn.'

Brooks was definitely inquisitive about the kind of school Prenderby would favour. 'What changes would you make?'

This brought a shrug by way of reply, and, 'I won't tell you, Brooks. But if I ever get the Headship, you'll see quickly enough, Probably you'd be shocked yourself?'

Brooks shook his head decidedly. 'I don't think I would. I've known you long enough to know that you have a very keen insight into schoolboy psychology. The boys know that too. That's why they hardly ever try to hide anything from you.'

'Which brings us right back to *Beasly*,' mused Prenderby, with a thoughtful scowl. 'I'm not sure I was right to let that young ass go home without straightening him out first. No telling *what* kind of trouble he may be in — for after all, to throw away the amount he's thrown away recently must involve some pretty deep roguery!'

With which verdict Brooks was inclined to agree . . .

3

A Worrying Telephone Call

The inn at which Mr. Prenderby had elected to spend his quiet and leisurely holiday nestled at the foot of a heather-clad hill not far from St. Andrew's Golf Course. Prenderby was a devotee of the game, and it was principally the course which had lured him so far for his break.

Outside the school staff, Prenderby never made friends very easily, but on this occasion he did meet up with a holidaying stockbroker: Edward Braith, a likeable, fifty-year-old man who had come to the inn for the same purpose as Prenderby. It was natural that they should go round together, more particularly so when they found they were both twelve-handicap men.

There is nothing like golf for forming firm friendships. Once off the course they began to stick together on local rambles, and excursions to places of interest. Prenderby overcame his usual reluctance to talk about himself in front of strangers, and expiated his views on the educational system and the improvement thereof.

'You see, Edward, I think the whole blasted thing's wrong! *Masters* are to blame, in the main — they forget to consider their pupils as human beings. To a great many masters, teaching is a job, and not a *purpose*. They're dependent on it for their means of livelihood, and their only concern is to knock as much of what they know into the thick skulls of the unwashed little blighters in their classes as possible. They forget that a child or an adolescent has a will and a personality of its own. To them, one boy is much like another. They are either good or bad, bright or dense — without any grey shades in between.'

'And how about yourself?' asked Braith.

'I have definite ideas. I don't expect for a minute you'll approve of them . . . but I'd welcome any chance to put them into practise. Firstly, I believe that boys are *people*.

'Most masters can be likened to glass-blowers — the glass-blower forces wind into the glass he's working on to mould it to the desired shape.

'Masters are the same. They force knowledge into the boys they're working on, to mould them into the desired shape. The trouble is that that shape never *varies*. It's a standard pattern. Boys are made to conform to it, whether the pattern suits them or not. Like the glass-blower, a master usually considers his material as nothing *but* material; instead of which, he's working with flesh and blood, and — if there *is* such a thing, which I've never decided — a soul. Whilst such stereotyped methods are in operation, we'll *never* turn out any really dominant leaders or personalities.'

Braith smiled. 'You're an idealist.'

'Perhaps I am.'

'Then, given a free hand, how would *you* change the system?'

Prenderby's crinkled eyes were no longer watching Braith.

'I'd take a school, any school, and give the boys complete *freedom*.'

'Complete freedom?' frowned Braith.

Prenderby nodded. 'I believe that's the solution. Freedom to go and come as they please, freedom to attend lessons or not to attend lessons, freedom to indulge in, or do without, sports. No compulsion of any kind. No canes. Freedom of speech, even to the extent of swearing. Freedom of movement.'

'You couldn't do it! You'd have a Bedlam on your hands.'

'At first, yes. But if the changes were gradual, I believe the boys would fall into the routine eventually.'

Braith shook his head slowly. 'It couldn't be done, man.'

'It *has* been done. There are a couple of schools in England today that are pioneering the trail. They have had markedly successful results. Their pupils are sincere and intelligent without sham or fake in them.'

Braith shrugged.

'I'd like to try it, anyway,' said Prenderby. 'Some day I *will* — trouble is that, even if I only make slight changes at first, I'm liable to be thrown out. St. Mark's is strictly hidebound. The Board hates anything new. I'll no sooner gain the Headmastership than I'll lose it, if I try to introduce any new rules and customs. Someday, if ever I get backing to start a revolutionary school of my own, I feel sure the methods I'd use would turn out clever and useful citizens!'

'And I feel just as strongly that you'd turn out rogues and immoral rascals. I'd hate to think of any son of mine going to such a school.'

'So would a lot of people who want their offspring cutting to pattern. But there are enough parents in the country with modernistic ideas to make such a school profitable — and more coming round to the same way of thinking each day.'

Braith laughed. 'If you ever do get the opportunity to put your theories into practise, I'll watch your career with considerable interest, John.'

'So will a great many other people,' smiled Prenderby. 'In the meantime I'll just have to go on being a housemaster;

and, as such, conforming to the rules already laid down by my superiors in my treatment of boys.'

They were seated in the lounge of the inn, settled in high-backed leather chairs with a fire in front of them and tankards of strong ale by their sides. There was a restful, old-world atmosphere about the place. Prenderby murmured:

'If you were wearing doublet and hose, I could almost imagine myself back in the Middle Ages.'

Braith nodded. 'No modern 'conveniences' here to destroy the illusion of peace,' he said; to which was given the lie almost immediately by the insistent ringing of the telephone.

It was followed by the entrance of the innkeeper.

'Mr. Prenderby? A telephone call for you, sir.'

Prenderby went into the bar to take it. The place was empty, with only the landlord wiping glasses at the sink to overhear the conversation. He made no effort to leave, and Prenderby didn't ask him to do so.

'Mr. Prenderby speaking — ?'

'Ah. This is Gilbert Soames — '

'*Soames* — ' said Prenderby, frowning. 'I can't seem to recall — '

'I am the guardian of one of the boys in your house, Mr. Prenderby . . .'

Prenderby remembered now. 'Of course. Beasly — am I right?'

'You are, Mr. Prenderby. I am indeed sorry to disturb you on your holiday — well-earned, I have no doubt — but I am somewhat concerned about my ward . . .'

Prenderby frowned at the mouthpiece. 'Has this any connection with the little matter Beasly and I discussed shortly before he left the school?'

'Then he did leave the school?'

'What? But *naturally* . . .'

'You see, Mr. Prenderby, I am worried. My ward was supposed to spend the first week of his holiday with an aunt of his in Bournemouth. That week passed, and when he failed to join me here in London for the rest of the break, I telephoned the aunt, and enquired if he intended to stay there. She, to my astonishment, told me he had not been there at all, that he had not turned up, and that she had taken it for granted that he had gone straight to me in London. That means that Eric has been *missing for a full eight days*. Ever since term's end. Of course, I at once telephoned the school to see if something had prevented him from leaving: an illness, or something of like nature. The caretaker informed me that he was not on the premises, and after enquiries had been made, he learned that the few pupils spending the holiday at the school had not seen Eric since breaking-up day. In my anxiety I thought it likely that *you* would know something of the matter. Accordingly, I obtained your holiday address from the caretaker, and took the liberty of telephoning you.'

Prenderby shook his head automatically. 'I'm sorry, but I have no more idea than you where Beasly can be. I can only tell you that he came to my study, at my request, shortly before he was due to leave, and he then had on hat and coat ready to catch the school bus. I detained him for a few minutes, and the last I saw of him he was apparently in a considerable hurry to rush away to the bus. At least, I assumed it was the bus for which he was rushing.'

Soames' rather fruity voice came through again.

'Yet he has not been home. Where can he *be*, Mr. Prenderby? Surely, as his housemaster, you have *some* idea — '

Prenderby grunted: 'None. My responsibility over the boys ends with the term. Nor am I a mind-reader. However, I have an inkling of why Beasly is missing. I may be wrong, but it is probably because of the unpleasant interview he had with me before he left.'

'Unpleasant interview?' queried Soames.

'Yes. I chanced to discover evidence that your ward had been gambling very heavily, and had lost a considerable sum of money. In addition, it seemed he was in debt to some bookmaker to the extent of more than thirty pounds. It was too near the term-end to do anything then. Dr. Wignall, our Headmaster, had already gone, and I could not take the responsibility of dealing with such a matter on my own shoulders. I therefore warned Beasly that he would have the music to face next term, when he returned.'

'But I fail to understand. How could my ward gamble away any sizeable sum of money when his allowance runs to no more than *a few shillings a week?*'

Prenderby said: 'That is what I myself would like to know, Mr. Soames.'

'And you think, being afraid to face the consequences of his actions at the beginning of next term, he has deliberately run away?'

'It seems possible.'

'But would he not have spent the holiday at home first, and left his disappearance until nearer the beginning of term?'

'Possibly — unless he thought I would communicate with you and inform you of his conduct.'

Soames muttered, almost inaudibly: 'Yes, yes . . . that must be it. I must admit I have always been rather hard on the boy. I felt he *needed* a stern hand. He has never been a particularly honourable youth. But something must be done — the question is *what*, Mr. Prenderby. What do you advise? Shall I wait a few days more to see if he turns up? Or shall I take other steps to have him found?'

'If Beasly has been missing for a week you must not delay a moment longer. You must inform the police at once. Place the entire matter in their hands. If he is to be found, *they* will find him. Acquaint the Metropolitan Force with his disappearance, and also the local constabularies in Munston and Branshoot.'

'What reason would I give? I would hesitate to tell them he had been — gambling — '

'Unless they ask you, you need tell them nothing.'

'Simply that he is missing?'

'Simply that. He can hardly have much money — personally, I feel that when what little he has is exhausted, he will turn up again. I wouldn't disturb myself unduly, Mr. Soames.'

'Thank you, Mr. Prenderby. I won't. And again, I'm sorry to have disturbed you on your holiday — but you understand — I am responsible for the boy, and — '

'I quite understand, and I am glad that you got in touch with me. I confess to being interested in my boys as persons, and not just as scholars with attached fees. I would be grateful for further information, when any comes to light.'

'I will let you know then, Mr. Prenderby. You will be at the same address and telephone number?'

'Until my return to school, yes.'

'Then you'll hear from me shortly. Good night.'

'Good night.'

Prenderby hung up, and for several minutes remained where he was, thinking. Beasly's vanishing trick had given him something of a shock. He knew his boys, and he would never have said that Beasly was the type to put himself to any inconvenience because of storms ahead. Beasly lacked the initiative to run away from trouble. He would have considered the trouble the lesser of two evils. He would have tried to brazen it out.

The far likelier theory was that Beasly,

despite a debt of thirty pounds, *still* had a considerable sum of money left; and, since trouble was ahead anyway, had decided to have a gay time of it with what remained, before going home.

Prenderby eventually returned to the lounge and his ale — which had gone flat — and Braith, who had gone to sleep during his absence. He didn't awaken Braith. He was thinking about Beasly, and about his own ideas for a Free School, and wondering how such an establishment would react upon a boy like the young gambler. Despite his faith in the plan, he felt uneasy. If he ever *did* get hold of a place of his own, he had an uneasy feeling that a few pupils like Beasly would ruin it entirely.

This wasn't the first time Beasly had been in some form of hot water. Beasly was an out-and-out blackguard. Judged by the standards of St. Mark's, Beasly was an utterly undesirable pupil. Hitherto, he had but narrowly escaped the sack. This latest exploit would probably mean the end for Beasly at St. Mark's.

Prenderby felt that Beasly should have

been expelled long ago, at the time of the thefts from the cricket pavilion. They had *known* that it was Beasly. But the element of doubt had been there, and Dr. Wignall was a just man. Pompously just.

So Beasly had remained.

About an hour later Braith woke up, yawned, and rubbed his eyes. 'The Devil! Have I been asleep? Sorry, old fellow. How about a round of golf before dinner?'

Prenderby glanced at the clock. He nodded. 'Just about time, I think; unless I get into that bunker at the Sixth again.'

Braith grinned. 'Surely you can't do it three times on the rim, old man?'

But Prenderby could — and *did*!

★　★　★

'The police seem to think he may have crossed to Ireland,' said Soames, over the phone. 'They have had a report of a lone schoolboy who might have answered to Eric's description, crossing. Trouble is, he seems to have vanished completely. They have asked the police in Northern

Ireland, and Eire, to make a thorough search for him.'

'And they've found no trace of him in England?'

'So far, no. They haven't given up, of course. They're prepared to say they're convinced he isn't in the vicinity of the school, at least. The main difficulty is that no one remembers which train he boarded, either at Munston or Branshoot. The ticket collectors say they couldn't be expected to remember one boy, no matter how pimply, from a total of some fifteen hundred boys and girls.'

'That's only to be expected, of course.'

'But it's been *five weeks* now — where the deuce can a boy of that age have *got* to for so long? He can't have had sufficient money to pay his way.'

'We can't be certain of that. However, the new term starts in a week or so, and he may quite likely turn up in the normal way. Or it is highly possible he may have told some of his schoolboy friends where he meant to go.'

'I sincerely hope that such is the case,' boomed Soames. 'I am a busy man, Mr.

Prenderby — very busy. Time is money, and this affair has already cost me a great deal of both.'

Braith, who was acquainted with the disappearance, looked at Prenderby as the latter came from the telephone.

'The boy's guardian again?'

Prenderby nodded. 'And in the dickens of a stew.'

'Then they haven't found him so far?'

'They haven't. He seems to have vanished without trace. No one even remembers seeing him.'

Braith grinned. 'The lad's only putting your own principles into operation. Complete *freedom*, you know.'

Prenderby laughed. 'I'm afraid Beasly isn't ready for complete freedom yet. He'd need to have the idea insinuated into his fat little head slowly and carefully.'

'I think a better idea could be insinuated into his fat little backside quickly and efficiently,' said Braith. 'And if I had anything to do with him, that's what would happen.'

And Prenderby said: 'That's what

probably will happen. But you can't blame the boy too much. From what I've gathered during these phone conversations with Soames, his trouble is most likely psychological, arising from absence of affection in his home life. A thing like that is apt to plant all kinds of silly ideas in an adolescent's mind . . . '

4

Mr. Prenderby is Asked for Help

Dr. Samuel Walter Wignall sighed heavily and, once again, studied the letter from Beasly's guardian. It was the first day of term, and normally a worrying time for the Head of a school as vast as St. Mark's. There were new pupils to be greeted and set on their courses with a kindly word and a terse summary of the rules. There were masters of infinite variety to welcome back; a new cook to be instructed in her duties; and a hundred other things. Most of them might have been quite ably performed by the staff members, but Dr. Wignall was a meticulous man, and acutely conscious of his importance in the general scheme of St. Mark's. He liked to be in on *everything*.

He had arrived back the day before to learn what he could regarding Beasly of the Fourth. He had learned precisely nothing. There was nothing to learn. The letter before him now was to tell him no fresh developments had taken place.

The local police were bewildered — but hardly more so than Dr. Wignall himself.

The affair had spoiled his entire holiday. He disliked any form of notoriety, particularly in connection with St. Mark's. The murder in the woods last term, and the fact that the victim had chanced to be a master's daughter, had occasioned a number of useful students to be withdrawn from the school. For days reporters had lurked about the district and bearded Mr. Gregg, the bereaved father, hounding out details of that fatal walk home alone by his daughter. One of them had actually had the downright impertinence to tackle Wignall himself and ask him if he considered the killer could be a member of the school staff.

It had all upset Dr. Wignall enormously. And now — this!

Beasly's strange disappearance had haunted him all that day. He had risen, as was his custom, at seven-thirty. Whilst he had shaved, he had been preoccupied with Beasly's past, unenviable record. Incidents had flitted across his mind, causing him to slice his left cheek rather nastily. A large cross of sticking plaster now adhered to the cut, detracting not a little from his dignity.

During breakfast, he had caught sight of a further report on what the newspapers had chosen to describe as the 'Vanishing Schoolboy Case'. It was brief, and tucked away under an account of a gruesome murder, but it would be read in millions of homes, nevertheless.

Dr. Wignall had been so annoyed he had spilt his soft-boiled egg on the cloth, a fact upon which his wife was quick to comment.

Later he had welcomed Mr. Prenderby and had talked for some time with him. Prenderby had acquainted him with the matter of Beasly's gambling activities, and Wignall had cautioned him not to let anyone else hear about it, or the papers would doubtless make hay!

Prenderby had then left, with an

assurance that he would question such of Beasly's intimate friends as he could find, and discover if *they* knew anything of the disappearance.

Then had come the cook, and then the new boys. Wignall had greeted the cook absently, telling her that he hoped she would be clean and observe strict happiness. The cook left, nettled and startled, unaware that what he had *meant* to say was that he hoped she would be happy and observe strict cleanliness. She couldn't, of course, know that he had a full mind.

The new boys had been greeted briefly, and despatched to their various house-masters.

And now the moment which Dr. Wignall had been dreading had arrived.

In answer to a tap at the door, he called: 'Come in.'

The door opened, and Mr. Gregg entered.

Mr. Gregg was on the plump side, semi-bald, with a face which had once been notable for its jovial redness. But since his daughter's death all that had changed. The redness was still there — but the joviality had been replaced by an expression which the school could not quite fathom.

The boys said, openly, that old Gregg was *loony*.

And indeed the staff inclined rather to that view themselves, preferring to say, in a milder vein: 'Yes, I fancy it *has* left him a bit *strange*, you know. Can't wonder, either. The poor girl was horribly messed about, I understand. Gregg was never the same man after he'd identified the body!'

It was because of this that Wignall had sent Gregg away from the school for a time. He had thought that a change in surroundings would restore the master to some of his old cordiality.

But one look at Gregg served to show that this had not resulted. It was Gregg's eyes, particularly, which were queer. Blank, almost lifeless — staring.

And his voice, which had once been hearty enough to bring an unruly form to order in a second, was now dull and toneless. The whole personality of the man was subdued.

Wignall sighed, and rose with out-stretched hand.

'Glad to see you again, Gregg. I hope you had a pleasant holiday?'

Gregg took his hand. There was something about his touch that Wignall didn't like. He removed his own hand rather too hastily, and coughed.

'I expect you'll be pleased to get back to your form?'

'Yes,' said Gregg quietly.

'Hmmm — of course. We've missed you — '

'Thank you.'

'But you really needed the rest to pull yourself together. It was a truly nasty shock — '

'*It still is*, Dr. Wignall,' said Gregg.

Wignall frowned. He didn't like that tone. After he'd been good enough to arrange for a paid holiday for Gregg — well, it was up to the man to get a grip on himself.

'Sit down, Mr. Gregg,' said Wignall, indicating a vacant chair.

Gregg sat down. Stiffly.

Wignall coughed again. Might as well

speak frankly to the man, he thought. But damn it, a grown man shouldn't go to pieces like this.

'Mr. Gregg, I had hoped that the break you've had would have cleared your mind a little of the tragedy of Miss Gregg's untimely death — '

Gregg winced, but Wignall pressed on firmly, refusing to pander to Gregg's misery.

' — and I trust sincerely that it has done so. Mr. Gregg, for your own sake, you must put aside all thoughts of the affair. You must take up your life exactly as you left it before the — er — before. Nothing can be accomplished by remembrance but your own ill-health . . . '

Gregg hadn't spoken, and didn't look as if he meant to.

'Put it *behind* you, Mr. Gregg. For your own sake — for the sake of St. Mark's, where you have been a master for so long.'

'I've tried,' Gregg replied, with a sudden shudder. 'But I — I can't seem to — '

'You must try again — harder. You

must rid yourself of these morbid thoughts, Gregg. It isn't like you.'

Gregg muttered, 'I'll try — '

Wignall stood up. 'Of course you will. And you'll succeed. I have little doubt that your association with us will be as long and happy as it has been so far.'

He managed to convey pleasantly enough, the idea that if Mr. Gregg *didn't* put morbid thoughts behind him, their association would be neither long nor happy.

He shook Gregg's hand again, and saw the master out.

When Gregg had gone, walking slowly and rigidly, Wignall shook his head and returned to his desk.

He was not interrupted until an hour later, when Prenderby came in to report on the failure of his mission to find out anything of value concerning the vanishing Beasly.

'His friends — the few he had — seem to think he had the definite intention of going to his aunt's home, as arranged, right up to the last minute — '

'*Which* last minute, Mr. Prenderby?'

said Wignall, irascibly.

'The last minute he was seen by anyone, soon after leaving my study. He then told Pritchet of the Fourth that he would write to him from Bournemouth. He was not seen after that by anyone.'

Dr. Wignall glanced once again at the letter in front of him. 'His guardian appears to think, from what you have told him of his ward's gambling tendencies, that the lad has tried to escape the consequences by running away?'

'It may be so, Dr. Wignall. I questioned Pritchet about the gambling. He assured me he knew nothing at all about it, but said that he had seen Beasly, several times, with four or five pounds in his wallet.'

'Did you ask the boy if he knew how Beasly came by those sums?'

'He seemed to be of the opinion that someone was giving a regular weekly amount to Beasly.'

'*Giving* it to him?'

'He wasn't certain, but that was what he had assumed.'

Dr. Wignall tapped tentatively at the

letter. 'It's plain he wasn't receiving the money from his guardian.'

'Quite plain.'

'Then *who* would be giving a schoolboy four or five pounds a week? And *why?*'

Prenderby shook his head. 'I have no idea, sir.'

Dr. Wignall grunted. 'This is a terrible affair, Prenderby. It could have — unwholesome repercussions. More so if it should become known that the boy was indebted to some — some bookmaker, for racing losses. Mr. Prenderby, I have often been struck by your astuteness in bringing to light various boys who have transgressed against the school rules. You are extremely perceptive — in short, I would be obliged to you if you could assist in any way in solving this mystery. If you could trace the bookmaker to whom the boy owed money, he might be able to throw some light — '

'I intend to do everything in my power, Dr. Wignall.'

'Of course. The police — ' He left the sentence unfinished, but his expression showed plainly what he thought of the police and their methods. He was prejudiced, for the police had worried him, and the school in general, at the time of the murder in the woods.

Prenderby glanced through the window.

'I understand. The presence of uniformed and plain-clothes police officials on the premises makes for a somewhat unsettling atmosphere.'

'Exactly. The sooner the matter is cleared up to their satisfaction, Prenderby, the sooner may we all relax. It is a most unsavoury business, but I have a feeling the solution is to be found somewhere in the school. Someone knows something which they are reluctant to tell. I am convinced of it.'

'I, too, have that feeling.'

Prenderby was still gazing from the window; Wignall now noticed this, and demanded: 'What is it, Mr. Prenderby?'

'I think the police are here now, sir. There is a uniformed constable at the gate, and a bowler-hatted man with him.'

'They have never left the place alone since the news of Beasly's disappearance reached them,' snapped Dr. Wignall. 'I had to suffer their questioning yesterday — but as yet they have learned nothing. Less than nothing.'

Prenderby nodded. 'They have little on which to work. I can only hope I will be more successful.'

'I am sure you will be.'

★   ★   ★

'How was Brighton and the uncle?' queried Prenderby, as Brooks met him in the corridor and shook his hand warmly.

'Ghastly,' confessed the junior master. 'I'm glad to be back, old man. The old idiot has forsaken his old bath-chair for one driven by a motor. He insisted on taking me for long country rides — only *I* had to slog away on a *pushbike* whilst he buzzed along quite merrily in his confounded contraption. It was positively loathsome. Once or twice I came close to speaking my mind, money or not. When I complained once that my legs were tired, he looked at me, said *his* weren't, started his infernal motor and travelled at top speed, and away we went again. I couldn't sit down for three days, I was so saddle-sore. Honestly. I've *still* got the blasted marks. I kept hoping he'd lose control of the chair, or his brakes would snap or something, and he'd run over a cliff — but damnit, no such luck.'

Prenderby sympathised.

Brooks eyed him. 'How did your jaunt in the Highlands go off? I bet you had a whale of a time.'

'I did, yes. It could have been better but for that trouble about Beasly, though.'

Brooks pricked up his ears. '*Beasly? Trouble?* What the devil has he done *now?* I remember you telling me about him gambling before we left . . . has he . . . ?'

'He's vanished,' murmured Prenderby. 'Those two large gentlemen you see in bowler hats, questioning the juniors, are from the county constabulary.'

Brooks looked mystified. 'I don't understand this. *How* has he vanished? Do you mean literally or figuratively?'

'I don't know. But he's gone so completely, I'm damned if I'm not

63

beginning to think it should be *literally*!'

Brooks whistled. 'When? Where?'

'Ever since term's end, apparently. He never turned up at his home.'

'By Jove! That sounds pretty serious to me.'

'It is pretty serious,' agreed Prenderby. 'Public schoolboy vanishing like that, has to be. Besides which, his guardian is a well-known London theatrical proprietor. The papers will play the thing up big if he isn't found shortly. They're already beginning to take notice. The publicity will be bad for the school — old Wignall's just about tearing his sidewhiskers from his face already.'

Brooks shook his head slowly. 'Sounds very queer to me. If he left here wearing school colours, coat and blazer — or did he?'

'Seemingly he did. A check showed those were the only clothes of his missing.'

'But if he had his luggage with him — ?'

'He didn't. That's the funny part. He'd sent it on to the station, and never picked it up from there. The police found it and held it. It looks as if he never left from the station at all.'

'As if something unforeseen cropped up to make him change his plans on the instant!' hazarded Brooks.

'But what could crop up in the life of a schoolboy, to warrant such a change?'

'That would depend on the schoolboy,' said Brooks. 'In the case of Beasly, after what you've told me about him — well, it could be a number of things.'

Prenderby stared moodily at the floor. 'Wignall's asked me to lend a hand, see if I can clear things up. How the devil he expects me to find anything where the police have failed, I have no idea . . . '

'I don't know so much,' murmured Brooks. 'I've seen you at work. You should have been a detective, old man. The way you ferret secrets out of those grubby little blockheads would make Sherlock Holmes himself green with envy.'

'I may have some luck when it concerns something that's happened on the premises,' acknowledged Prenderby. 'But when a kid vanishes, and the police are stumped, and he has the whole of England to hide in — well, I imagine that it would tax the ingenuity of even Sherlock Holmes. Still, I'll try — '

'Good man. And if you need a Doctor Watson — let me know. I'm stupid enough to be a stimulus to you, aren't I?'

''Am I not?',' corrected Prenderby, mechanically. 'I'll let you know if I need any help. Though God knows where I'm going to start.'

He started at that moment, but his present start was one of surprise. He said: 'What the . . . what the hell! That can't be a member of the force — can it?'

Brooks turned and witnessed that which had caused Penderby's astonishment. Proceeding towards them from the direction of the gates was a stocky, greasily-complexioned individual, attired in a check suit and a Derby hat. Projecting from the corner of his mouth hung a limp cigar, unlighted. His hands were driven into his trouser pockets, holding his jacket open, and revealing a florid waistcoat across which hung a large watch-chain.

Prenderby grunted: 'I've seen that character before — and I think it was in the taproom at the Blue Boar in Munston. I may be mistaken, but if I'm not, he's one of the old-style bookmakers. He certainly dresses the part, anyway.'

The showy individual had veered in their direction, and now drew level and halted, scrutinising them keenly.

'Good afternoon. I'm looking for the 'Ead of this Collige. A Dr. Wignall.'

Prenderby muttered, 'Is it urgent? The Headmaster is busy at the moment. Possibly I can help you?'

'Who're you?' said the man suspiciously.

'My name is Prenderby. I'm the master of North House.'

'Oh. Then it concerns a lad in your 'ouse, Mr. Prenderby. A young fellow by the name of Beasly. The one that's missing. I suppose you'll be as much good to me as the 'Ead.'

Prenderby nodded. 'I'm sure I will. If you'll step along to my study, we can talk without being disturbed.'

Brooks looked hesitant. As if he was

unsure whether to intrude on the discussion or not. Prenderby settled the question for him.

'See you later, Brooks, old man. This way, Mr. — ?'

'Grey. Barry Grey.'

'This way, Mr. Grey.'

★　★　★

'Now then, Mr. Grey,' said Prenderby, lighting a pipe and sitting back behind his desk. 'Have you some knowledge of the missing junior?'

Grey shook his head, from which he had neglected to remove his hat. The unlighted cigar still dangled from his lips. 'I want to know where the lad is meself,' he grunted. 'I 'ave a little matter of thirty quid owin' to me . . . '

Prenderby had suspected that might be the case. Now his eyes hardened a little, and he drew deeply on the pipe.

'I was aware that Beasly was indebted to that extent. Then you are a bookmaker?'

'That I am. 'E's been layin' five or six

quid a week with me, or 'ad been up to the end of the term. The week before the school broke up, 'e backed 'eavily — lost the lot. 'E could only pay me three quid, but 'e said that 'e'd let me 'ave the rest without fail before 'e went home. Thirty quid odd, 'e owed. 'E said 'e wouldn't fail me, like I've said; and I told 'im if he did, I'd come up here an' see his 'Eadmaster.'

'And here you are,' finished Prenderby.

''Ere I am. And I'm waitin' to 'ear who's going to pay my money. If 'e's missin, his guardian'll have to.'

Prenderby leaned forward. 'Are you aware that you've been committing a very serious offence by accepting bets from a person under age?' he said, his voice steely for all its drawl.

Grey smiled. 'That I am. But I don't suppose your 'Ead would care to report the matter to the police. It'd not do for the name of the school if 'e did. Am I right?'

Prenderby sucked at his pipe and nodded. 'Quite right. But you're forgetting one thing — that a minor's debts aren't legal, Mr. Grey. You are not entitled to claim one penny. The foolish boy would probably have paid you himself had he had the money, to preserve his secret. Now — you have simply wasted your time coming here. I will, of course, *mention* the matter to the Headmaster. It will be for him to decide what is to be done *in your own case* — '

Grey looked startled. "Ere — '

'And now I think you'd better go. Good day.'

'But listen — well, on second thoughts, I think it'd be as well if you didn't bother the 'Ead. I've been thinkin', an' it seems to me . . . '

'You should have thought *before* you came here. Good day, Mr. Grey.'

5

Mr. Prenderby Notices an Unpleasant Smell in Top Attic

The first three days of the new term passed without any added light being thrown on the missing schoolboy. It seemed that Beasly had vanished into the very air, and there were a great many puzzled frowns.

Most of the boys expected he'd show up sooner or later. One or two thought he wouldn't. They felt it would go down in history as one of those famous unsolved mysteries.

'People,' said the sergeant from the village police, 'do vanish like this, y'know. Without leaving a trace. In the meantime, we're keepin' an eye on the station to see if anybody enquires at lost property for that luggage belonging to the lad. We can't do no more than that at this end.'

The school settled down to routine.

The new cook was functioning as cooks should function, to everyone's satisfaction; the new boys had been ragged and japed without mercy; a fresh outbreak of scribbling in the lavatories was underway; and Mr. Gregg, whilst performing his duties competently, still prowled — the only word for it — until all hours of the night, with that rather peculiar look in his eyes.

Beasly continued absent. His name was tactfully dropped from the roll. His guardian had ceased to worry, and had left the matter in the hands of the authorities. Even the papers began to tire of the news. It was no longer mentioned. Beasly had become just another missing person.

Only Mr. Prenderby retained any interest in the matter. And he kept his thoughts to himself.

Dr. Wignall had seen fit to report the matter of Barry Grey and his iniquities to the local police station. From there had sallied forth Constable Hodgman, a stern look upon his face, determined to put the fear of God into Barry Grey.

On being confronted with his crimes, Mr. Grey promptly denied all knowledge of any gambling transactions with junior schoolboys, and refuted the suggestion that Beasly had owed him the sum of thirty pounds, with dignity.

'*Prove* it?' he had said, and Constable Hodgman, having been informed that it was merely Prenderby's word against the word of Mr. Grey, couldn't.

He retired in good order; for if he had not made a case he had at least fulfilled his purpose, which had been principally to make Mr. Grey realise it was unwise to allow junior schoolboys to contract gambling debts.

On the fourth day of term, Mr. Prenderby was secretly amused, whilst gazing from his study window into the Quadrangle, to see Pritchet of the Fourth negotiating some business with Mills Major and Bagshot of the Fifth.

Pritchet, after a cautious glance round, took from his pocket a large packet of Woodbines. Mills Major grabbed them hastily and stowed them away. Their voices drifted upwards:

'Thanks, Pritchet. Nobody saw you getting them in the village?'

'Nobody at all — '

'Good kid,' muttered Bagshot. 'I've been bursting for a smoke ever since yesterday evening. Thanks, Pritch.'

They turned to go, and Pritchet yelled: 'You didn't pay me yet — '

'Some other time, kid. Chalk it up,' said Bagshot. 'Remind us next week. We happen to be a bit short.'

'But look here . . . '

'Don't quibble, Pritchet,' said Mills Major, with a loftiness becoming to a senior addressing a junior. 'My friend Bagshot said *chalk it up*.'

'But I want — '

'What you want is nothing to what you'll get if you don't stop arguing the point,' snorted Bagshot. 'We've been good enough to allow you to fetch cigarettes for us, haven't we? And you repay us by squalling about a miserable sum of money. Which,' he added, as an afterthought, 'we haven't got anyway. If we'd had enough to get them ourselves, do you think we'd have bothered *you?*'

'Quite,' nodded Mills. 'We're a bit short. Got into a game of cards with Burnley of Morefell on the train back to school. Lost quite a packet. Now buzz off, you grubby little fag, or I'll boot you.'

Recognising the danger signal, and realising that Mills would pay up eventually anyhow, Pritchet withdrew with an injured air.

Bagshot smiled, glanced briefly at Mills.

'The boxroom?' said Bagshot.

'The *top* boxroom,' clarified Mills Major. 'Without delay.'

And, turning with common accord, they vanished, round the corner of the building!

⋆   ⋆   ⋆

Prenderby sighed. He really didn't wish to hike all the way to the top boxroom to stop two seniors indulging in a quiet cigarette. But unfortunately he was a man with a clear sense of duty. Whatever his own views were with regard to freedom for schoolboys, he was unable to forget

75

that the Board of Governors and his Headmaster looked to him to stamp out such things whilst he was Housemaster of North.

He strolled easily towards the door of his study, out, and along the corridor towards the stairs.

To understand his subsequent actions it is necessary to have a brief outline of the topography of North House:

At the end of the Masters' corridor stands Big Hall. Across Big Hall, and beyond the classrooms, may be found a double staircase which runs up to the Fifth Form corridor. To the right of the Fifth Form corridor is yet another staircase, connecting with the Junior studies. The third floor houses Second, Third, and Fourth Form dormitories.

A narrow door opening off the Fourth Form corridor leads to a flight of wooden stairs, very steep and very treacherous. At the top of these stairs are six boxrooms, where the boxes of the juniors are stored during term-time.

These rooms are connected one with the other by means of arch-like openings without doors. In the far one there is the *final* staircase which leads to the topmost gable attic of the house. This staircase is so steep and badly constructed that it might almost be mistaken for a stepladder.

While Mr. Prenderby was climbing the second staircase down below, Mills Major and Bagshot were laboriously ascending the final staircase leading to the top attic.

Top Attic was the time-honoured place for any furtive behaviour on the part of the North House pupils. A hidden watcher might often have seen cautious, creeping figures repairing to the attic late at night. Secret smokers, fags, those bent on reading (in peace) pornographic literature; and, once a month, at midnight, mysterious cowled figures: the members of the Black Circle, a long-established St. Mark's' junior Society.

Mills Major and Bagshot Minor had chosen the attic to smoke their first cigarettes of the term. Unaware that Mr. Prenderby was already hot on their trail, they scrambled into the dusty attic, home of battered and unspliced cricket bats, fives bats in the last stages of disrepair, threadbare boxing gloves, gutless tennis rackets, broken chairs and tables, and a thousand and one other heterogeneous articles discarded by both recent and long-gone generations of schoolboys.

They kicked a space amongst the wreckage, and lit up.

'Watch what you do with your fag-end,' warned Mills. 'You remember what Prenderby said about us smoking here when he last caught us. Didn't seem to mind the smoking so much as the possibility of our starting a fire. He'll come down heavy if he finds fag-ends dropped all over again.'

'*Good* sort, old Prenny,' said Bagshot, blowing a cloud of blue smoke into the dusty air. 'Rather be in his house than any of the others.'

They dragged at their weeds in silence for a moment. Then Mills sniffed disgustedly, and looked about him.

'I say, Baggy — there's the deuce of a niff coming from somewhere . . . '

'I noticed it when we came up,' agreed

Bagshot, wrinkling his nostrils. 'Didn't like to say anything in case it was you, old bean. Mean to say it *isn't*?'

'Damned if it is. Phew — it's jolly strong, Baggy. Like — like a dead rat.'

'Maybe a bird's flown in and died here?' suggested Bagshot.

Mills stood up. 'Whatever it is, it's too much for me. Come on — we'll finish these off in the boxrooms below.'

The odour up there was really nauseating. And it showed no signs of diminishing. Accordingly, the two Fifth Formers headed for the stairs again and made their way down . . .

. . . in time to bump into Mr. Prenderby, who was standing in the doorway waiting for them.

'Small world, Mills, Bagshot, isn't it?' he observed, as the luckless two hove into view.

They halted with a startled gasp. Mills thrust his smoke behind his back. Bagshot cupped his and placed his hand carefully into his trouser pocket.

Mills contrived to drop his cigarette and grind his heel back onto it.

Prenderby watched these actions genially.

Volumes of smoke began to issue from Bagshot's pocket. The Housemaster murmured: 'You appear to be on fire, Bagshot.'

Bagshot, realising further subterfuge was useless, withdrew his cigarette, dropped it, and put his foot on it.

Prenderby motioned them forward, held out his hand.

'I'll take the rest of your supplies.'

'We haven't any — '

'I trust you were not about to say you hadn't any more?' said Prenderby, quickly. 'If so, I shall be extremely annoyed. I am fully aware that you have a further eighteen cigarettes in your pockets.'

Mills flushed and produced the Woodbines, which Prenderby thrust into his own pocket. He then regarded them gravely.

'Mills and Bagshot — I caught you two up here last term, didn't I?'

'Yes, sir.'

'Didn't I warn you then that you would

be punished for any repetition of your offence?'

'Yes, sir,' nodded Bagshot, glumly.

'Then so you shall — I think a hundred lines will meet the case, due by roll-call tomorrow. I don't think I'm being, unduly harsh — '

They were both relieved. They knew that any other master would have taken a far more serious view of smoking, which was strictly prohibited for both juniors and seniors. Prenderby saw their expressions and added, sternly:

'Next time the punishment will be a lot worse. And — you can tell Pritchet that if I catch him sneaking any more fags into the school, there'll be a licking for *him*. Understand?'

He spoke briskly, and they understood. They nodded.

Prenderby said: 'All right. Away you go — and confine your smoking to the holidays in future.'

Glad to escape so lightly, they made haste to leave the boxrooms. Prenderby heard them go, then turned to leave himself.

A sudden thought made him turn back again. They'd been up in the top boxroom, which was loaded with highly-flammable rubbish. It would be as well, he thought, to make sure they hadn't dropped any lighted matches or glowing cigarette ends.

He mounted the stairs with agility. And at once he became aware of the peculiar stench which lurked all about him.

'Whoof!' grunted Prenderby, putting fingers to nose. 'What the hell — ?'

That there was something up in the top attic was only too evident. Where there was a smell, there had to be a cause for it. Prenderby, albeit reluctantly, felt it was a duty to determine what was *causing* that dreadful pong, so that a stop could be put to it.

An odour like that couldn't be healthy, and though the attic was seldom used, there was no reason why it shouldn't be free of unpleasant stenches.

Prenderby glanced round. The only light up there was admitted by the small window above him. The rest of the place lay in fust and darkness.

Prenderby took matches from his pocket and lit one. He held the flickering light above his head and peered towards the stack of rubbish.

The floor in front of a pile of broken chairs was stained with some liquid which had trickled, and then congealed.

At the moment it was black — Prenderby thought it might have once been the dregs of some old inkwell. And then his eyes fell upon a broken cricket bat which lay nearby. The splintered base of this was stained with the same black liquid. Prenderby bent curiously —

He stared long and hard, frozen, into immobility.

The match burned down to his fingers . . .

'Damn and blast!' said Prenderby, and dropped it hastily to suck his scorched thumb.

After a moment he lit a second match. Bending as he was, the smell hit him with far greater strength. He grunted: 'Ugh!'

He stood up, and struck his third match. He pushed an old desk aside and forced a way through to the back of the pile of chairs . . .

Now the reason for the stain was evident. So was the reason for the dried skin and hair on the base of that old cricket bat.

Beasly had turned up again.

Or at least, the corporeal shell of Beasly had turned up. Where his soul had fled, Prenderby would not have been prepared to state. A glance served to show that it had indeed fled, however.

'Well,' Prenderby told himself, to gain time for thought, 'this *is* a surprise! The lad was here all the time.'

There could be little doubt from the state Beasly's body was in that it had been lying there since the time of his sudden disappearance. It presented an unsavoury spectacle: jammed backwards, face-up, amongst the wreckage of a half-dozen chairs and desks. The head lolled back aimlessly, the face was constricted into a blackened mask of fright. The eyes were open, protruding, staring, anguished . . . the side of the head was battered into a messy pulp . . .

Prenderby looked at the bat again, then

at the dried and blackened pimples on the dead boy's features, then at the smashed temple. It was Beasly all right. Prenderby murmured:

'Somebody hit a boundary that time. And it's to be hoped Dr. Wignall's good lady has a bottle of smelling salts in stock. Wiggy's going to need them, I think.'

At this point it would have been natural for Prenderby to have left the room and reported the find without further delay. But he didn't. He lingered, fascinated by his first body. It had always been his ambition to find one, and here one was. As gruesome a corpse, too, as was ever found within the pages of some lurid thriller.

The black, suffused face intrigued Prenderby. It didn't quite hit the same note as the battered head.

He lit yet another match, and bent forward to make a closer examination.

After a moment he drew upright again, murmured: 'No doubt of it. He was *strangled* — probably first. Then his head was battered in with the willow — why? Make *certain* he was dead?'

85

That seemed the logical conclusion.

A glimpse of white attracted his attention. He stooped and picked up a blood-soaked handkerchief. With the aid of the match he studied it carefully.

F.C.

Those were the initials in one corner. He took a scrap of old impot paper from a pile nearby, wrapped the clue up. Replaced it in his pocket.

The glitter of bright metal flashed in the light of the match he held; pushing aside a chair, he retrieved from beneath it a small, automatic cigarette lighter. The top of this was open, and the wick had burned down to nothing.

Prenderby placed it thoughtfully in his pocket for future reference.

Three more minutes dragged by whilst he hunted the attic. But, as he ground the fifteenth match underfoot, he was forced to admit that the possibilities were exhausted.

Nothing more had presented itself for collection.

Armed with his two clues, Prenderby left the attic and the body, and returned thoughtfully to his study.

He was aware that he was depriving the police of clues by pocketing the only two things which might have meant something. And yet, he felt that those clues would prove more valuable in his *own* hands. He might, in the case of the lighter, trick someone into an admission of ownership. Whereas, in police hands, the lighter would not be acknowledged by anyone, particularly if it belonged to the murderer.

Prenderby put through a phone call to the police, then proceeded at once to his Headmaster's study.

Dr. Wignall was engaged on the task of correcting some essays in Greek, atrocities for which the Sixth Form was held responsible. He looked up as Prenderby entered.

He was not pleased at being disturbed. But, with as much grace as he could muster, he said: 'Yes? What is it, Mr. Prenderby?'

'I thought you'd like to know sir — I've found Beasly.'

'Beasly? Of your — *when? Where?*'

'A few minutes ago. In the boxroom — he's — *dead!*'

6

Mr. Prenderby Breaks Disturbing News

No doubt Prenderby could have found a gentler method of breaking that startling piece of information, had he tried. But he had never been a man to beat round the bush.

On the whole, Dr. Wignall took it well. Apart from the large blot which dropped from his pen to the essay he was correcting when his hand gave the first jump of shock, he controlled his feelings admirably.

'He has been for some time,' Prenderby added as Wignall looked at him in anguish.

It must always be a nerve-shattering experience for a headmaster to hear of the death of one of his pupils on the premises. Boys of school age are not *supposed* to die — parents are apt to lay the blame on the school itself when they do so, no matter what the *cause* of death.

Two years ago, Smith-Williams of the Third had fallen downstairs and broken his neck. His inconsolable parents had stated quite bluntly that they wished they had never sent him to St. Mark's. They averred that had they chosen some other school, the accident would never have *happened*. Which was true enough, but hardly fair to St. Mark's.

But, death from natural causes does occur, Wignall told himself. If Beasly was dead, that was that. He was unaware that the biggest shock was yet to come. The cause of Beasly's death.

He looked at Prenderby, and said: 'What was wrong with him? Why did he die, Mr. Prenderby?'

Prenderby still saw no occasion for bush-beating. So he said:

'This is going to be a shock to you, sir. The fact is, he was *murdered*!'

Wignall half-rose from his chair, and stayed like that; his eyes fixed unbelievingly upon the North Housemaster, his knees slightly bent, his hands gripping the edge of the desk. He remained where he was, despite the discomfort of his position, seemingly suspended by invisible wires.

'I — no — you mean — killed by violence?'

'I'm afraid so, sir.'

The wires snapped and Wignall thumped audibly back into his swivel chair.

He passed a hand over his brow. His face was pale.

'Tell me the rest of it, Prenderby.'

'It was quite a shock to me, sir. I had no idea Beasly was up in the boxroom in my own house. I went up there in search of two seniors whom I had reason to believe were smoking. I punished them, and sent them down below. Then I thought it would do no harm to make a quick investigation of the boxroom — I was afraid of fire, you understand. I noticed a rather strong odour up there, and this led me to make a search for its cause.

'I found Beasly behind a pile of chairs. He had been strangled and then, apparently, his head had been battered badly with an old cricket bat. I left him there and came to report.'

Dr. Wignall drew a deep breath. When news of this leaked out he foresaw a greatly-reduced roll at St. Mark's.

'What can we *do*, Mr. Prenderby?' he asked weakly.

'There is only one thing *to do*,' Prenderby told him. 'Send for the police as quickly as possible.'

'Yes, yes — I suppose — '

'I have already sent for them, Dr. Wignall. They should be here very soon.'

Wignall stood up and paced feverishly towards the window.

'This must be kept quiet, Prenderby . . . '

'I'm afraid that is a question for the police to decide, sir.'

'But the good name of the school — '

'They will hardly be likely to consider that where a murder case is concerned. There will be the fullest investigation, I expect. I myself would say Beasly had been dead in the boxroom since the end of last term. That must naturally make the police's job a good deal harder.'

'But who could have done this thing? Who could have had reason to kill a junior schoolboy in such a foul manner?'

Prenderby frowned.

'I'm afraid the police will jump to the conclusion that the murderer is either a pupil here or a member of the staff, scholastic or domestic. No stranger could have known about, or had access to, the top boxroom. Beasly was obviously murdered by someone *actually in the school*, someone we all know and have spoken to often.'

Dr. Wignall turned away from the window again and slumped back into his chair.

There was a momentary silence, and Prenderby sensed he would have to help Dr. Wignall pull himself together.

'I think the boy's guardian should be informed as soon as possible, Dr. Wignall,' he murmured. 'Perhaps you would prefer that I telephoned him . . . ?'

Wignall looked up. 'Please do — and then — remain here with me until the police arrive, Prenderby. I will be very grateful for your assistance. I hardly feel in any state to deal with them myself at the moment. Perhaps *you* would be good enough to show them to the boxroom — '

Prenderby nodded as he picked up the telephone. He knew that Wignall had always had a horror of death in any form. There had once been a sparrow which had broken its neck flying into the telephone wires at the school. It had fallen on the steps of North House, and Wignall had been the first to see it as he was coming over to see Prenderby on a matter of school routine.

Prenderby remembered how pale and disgusted his face had been as he came in and said: 'There's a dead sparrow on the steps. Be good enough to ask the porter to *remove* it, Mr. Prenderby. I — I detest — '

He had broken off quickly, realising he was revealing a weakness. Prenderby had gone out and thrown the sparrow into a neighbouring field himself.

If Wignall's reaction to a dead sparrow were such, what would it be to a dead schoolboy? And one who had met a violent death at the hands of some other person?

Prenderby felt almost sorry for Dr. Wignall as he made the call to Beasly's guardian.

'Mr. Soames?'

'Speaking — '

'Mr. Prenderby of North House, St. Mark's. I'm afraid I have some very bad news — '

'About my ward?'

'Very tragic news, I'm afraid, Mr. Soames . . . you must brace yourself for a considerable shock . . . '

Soames sounded irritable: 'Come, come, Mr. Prenderby. I am not a child!'

'I'm afraid your ward is dead, Mr. Soames.'

'What? Did you say — dead?'

'Not only dead, but — murdered.'

There was a silence at the other end. And then:

'I see, Mr. Prenderby. When and where was this discovered?'

'The boy was in a disused room on the school premises. I found the body myself a few minutes ago. He had been brutally strangled — had been dead for some time.'

'Have you informed the police?'

'We have. If you could manage to come down tomorrow, Mr. Soames — '

'I'm sorry. I have some very important business to attend to. I am afraid I will be unable to make the journey at all. Perhaps you could tell me the details by *letter?*'

Prenderby was not a sentimentalist. But he could not but be incredulous at the perfectly matter-of-fact way in which Soames had taken the news. He frowned.

'I really think — '

'It would be utterly impossible for me to make the journey, Mr. Prenderby. This whole affair has been a considerable source of trouble and wasted time so far . . . if the boy is dead, there is little I can do to help him now — '

He actually sounded relieved. Prenderby grunted: 'When the police give their permission, I take it you will desire the body sent to you for burial?'

There was a pause. 'Would it be possible for burial to take place from the school premises? If so, I should be extremely grateful — ?'

Prenderby cupped the mouthpiece and

looked at Dr. Wignall. 'The boy's guardian asks if we would bury Beasly from here . . . '

Wignall frowned. Then shrugged. 'If he wishes it so.'

Prenderby lifted the phone again. 'Dr. Wignall agrees that burial shall take place from here. There will be a representative of your family, I presume?'

'I'm afraid not. My wife cannot come, she is not very well, and I will be busy — but if you will have the bills sent to me, and accept a sum for your trouble — '

'It will be no trouble, Mr. Soames,' said Prenderby, very icily. 'Doubtless you will hear from the police in due course. I am sorry to have been the purveyor of such bad news — '

'Quite, quite — then that is all we can do for the moment?'

'For the moment, yes. Goodbye, Mr. Soames.'

'Goodbye, Mr. Prenderby. And thank you for calling.'

Prenderby put the phone down as the line went dead.

Dr. Wignall said: 'How did he take the news?'

'I am quite sure he *welcomed* it,' said Prenderby, grimly. 'I hardly think Mr. Soames is a type of man I'd care to know. He actually sounded glad to hear that responsibility for the junior's actions had been lifted from his shoulders!'

'He is not coming down to the school?'

'He feels no necessity to make the journey.'

'But for the *funeral* — ?'

'He is leaving the entire thing to us, and we are to send on the bills. He will not be present, nor will any member of his family.'

Dr. Wignall said: '*Good Heavens!* Has the man no affection for his ward?'

'Quite the reverse, I should say . . . ' Prenderby muttered, ' . . . and not as surprised as he might have been, either.'

★   ★   ★

A coterie of constables on pushbikes turned into the gates of St. Mark's and cycled smartly across to the School

House, led by the sergeant and Constable Hodgman, his best man. Prenderby was waiting for them on the steps, and hailed them as they drew near.

'North House, gentlemen. Dr. Wignall has asked me to show you the — scene of the crime.'

Accompanied by the force, he struck off for North House. The curious eyes of some three dozen mingled juniors and seniors followed their progress across the quadrangle.

Something was plainly up. As Pritchet said to his crony:

'It isn't often one sees bunches of bobbies bargin' about in this blessed concentration camp!'

Pritchet was very fond of alliterative remarks. He considered himself rather clever at stringing them together.

'Probably something to do with Beasly,' said Smail, eyeing the retreating blue-clad backs. 'But what the deuce have they sent along such a lot of bobbies for, I'd like to know?'

They were still further amazed when a short time later a blue and roomy car arrived. Smail recognised it as the official police car from Branshoot, the nearest C.I.D. headquarters to the school. Four plain-clothes men alighted, and vanished into North House.

Grass of the Fourth was the first to bring any news.

'I say,' he burst out excitedly, joining Pritchet and Smail, 'they're all up in the *top boxroom*, clumping about like a herd of blessed elephants. I can hear them arguing about something up there — I say, I wonder what's gone *wrong?*'

There were many others who wondered that. But they were doomed to disappointment that day. For no announcement was made.

All they could learn was that something covered with a white sheet had been taken down to an ambulance on a stretcher. This gave them plenty of cause for surmise. And by bedtime that night, they knew there was a constable on guard at the foot of the stairs leading to top attic; and that as far as Pritchet could ascertain, no one was allowed to go up there.

It was an excited and uneasy night for the school. That white-covered object on the stretcher spoke for itself. But no one was able to discover who was missing from his accustomed place. The thought that it might be Beasly, left there since end of term, didn't occur to them.

Rake of the Fifth expressed the hope it might be old Wignall. But that theory was disproved when Dr. Wignall was seen pacing nervously up and down under the elms that evening.

★ ★ ★

Nothing further happened until the following morning, just after first break. Then each classroom was visited by a plain-clothes detective, who had a few words to say.

'I want you boys to listen to me carefully. A very tragic and startling business has come to light concerning Beasly of the Fourth Form, the junior who was missing.

'Any boy who has been in the top attic of North House since *the last day of last*

100

term, or *upon* *that* *day*, must step forward now! There is nothing to fear — I merely wish to ask a few simple questions. But the matter is serious, and any boy who tries to evade an admission of having been in the attic, and is later proved to have been there, will meet with very unpleasant consequences. Now — ?'

The staff were asked the same thing.

And during the afternoon, those who admitted to having been in the attic since the final day of term, and upon that day, were assembled in the Headmaster's study.

There were no representatives of the Junior School. But of the Fifth there were Mills and Bagshot, who could not have denied having been there anyway, since Mr. Prenderby had caught them on the spot. There was Baxter of the Sixth, a very popular prefect. Of the boys, those were the only ones who had admitted being in the attic.

None of the domestic staff had come forward. But quite a surprising number of the masters were present.

Prenderby himself, of course; Brooks;

Frank Chester of the Third Form, East House; and Mr. Clannson, the sports master.

The detectives already had Prenderby's story; they took the others quickly.

Mills and Bagshot confessed their object in visiting the boxroom, and said they had noticed the smell. They were readily ruled out — the body had lain there a considerable time.

Baxter of the Sixth said he had been to the boxroom about four weeks ago, *two weeks after the school had broken up*. He had been one of the unfortunates who was spending the break at school, and had discovered that a volume of humour stories, which he had intended to read, had vanished.

He remembered throwing some old books into top attic about two weeks before end of term, and had wondered if he had also thrown away the humour stories by mistake.

He had been to the boxroom, and had rooted through the piles of discarded books. He had found the volume he wanted, and left again at once.

'Did you notice any peculiar odour at that time?'

'No, sir.'

Baxter was dismissed, and Brooks took his place. Brooks said he had been up to the boxroom on the last day of term, early in the morning. He had been there to dump an old cricket bat for which he had no further use.

'You did not observe anyone up there, or in the vicinity of the room?'

'No one ... oh, of *course* — Mr. Chester was on his way up as I was coming down. I passed him and said a good morning to him.'

Frank Chester nodded. 'That's true. My object in going up to the boxroom was similar to Mr. Prenderby's. I was aware that one of the boys in my form had a collection of pornography, saved during the term. I had reason to believe he had hidden these somewhere, out of the way. I hoped to find them in the *boxroom* ... '

'I understood your house was East House?'

'That is so. I am Master of the Third Form there.'

'Then how did you come to believe the boy had hidden anything in the boxroom of *North House?*'

'I was informed ... ' He spoke uneasily.

'Informed? By whom?'

'By — by one of my pupils. He reported the affair to me, and claimed he had seen the boy in question making for the North House boxroom with a bundle of books under his arm.'

'I see. If you will give me the name of the boy concerned I will verify that, Mr. Chester. Did you *find* the literature in question?'

'No. I spent some time searching, but of course I could not hope to cover *all* the ground. Perhaps the boy's destination was not, after all, the boxroom ... '

7

Mr. Prenderby Assists the Law

Clannson, the Sports Master, was next to be interrogated. It appeared that Clannson had been up to the top boxroom only the previous day. His object had been to dump a set of cricket pads which had seen their best days.

'Yes, I did notice the smell up there,' he admitted when questioned. 'But I didn't really have time to investigate; and anyway, I thought it might have been caused by musty books or some rubbish of that nature.'

The inspector in charge of the investigation scratched his head.

'What I don't understand is *why* all this rubbish is dumped in a boxroom! What's the reason? You have dustbins, I take it?'

Prenderby took it upon himself to explain.

'The dustbins are really commandeered

by the domestic staff. It's their job to dispose of anything the boys don't want, that is left out for them. But one can't dispose of old desks and chairs in that fashion. Besides, things dumped in the top boxroom can often be made use of again.'

'That's true,' nodded Clannson. 'Take the cricket pads — those were earmarked for the village boys' club. Sooner or later I'd have had them along here asking if there was any old gear to be had. I would then have let them take whatever they wanted from top attic. There's a shortage of dustbin space, and it's become natural to dump anything fairly large in top attic now.'

The investigation revealed nothing further, and the assembled boys and masters were dismissed.

Prenderby remained behind with the inspector. As the finder of the corpse he had special privileges.

The Inspector shook his head slowly. 'I learned exactly nothing from all that. I think they were *all* telling the truth — and of course, it's highly likely the real guilty person wouldn't have owned to being up there anyhow. If one suspect does emerge, it would be that fellow — what's his name? *Chester*. He was, to the best of everyone's knowledge, the *last* in the attic on the last day of term. I think we can assume that the junior was murdered on the *last* day, and not during the holidays themselves.'

'Perhaps it would be as well to ascertain the last one to see Beasly alive on that day?'

The Inspector nodded. 'I think that must be our next step.'

'Then I can assist you there. I myself saw Beasly in my study at about ten-forty-five on breaking-up day. Taking that as a starting point, it should be easy enough to determine if he was seen later, and by whom . . . '

It was even easier than they had hoped. Individual enquiries elicited the fact that Montague of the Third Form, East House, had been the last to see Beasly alive. Except, of course, for the murderer.

'I'd taken over some books for Beasly, to North House,' Montague told them, when brought to the Headmaster's study.

'Books?' questioned Prenderby.

'Er — yes, sir. Some — some books Beasly was buying from me.'

The Inspector interrupted: 'Your name has been given to me by your form master, Mr. Chester. He states that he followed you to North House that morning, suspecting you of carrying pornographic literature to hide in the top attic. Is this so?'

'Carrying what, sir?' said Montague, puzzled.

'Undesirable books,' explained Prenderby.

'Oh!' The junior coloured. 'I — well, yes, sir.'

The Inspector nodded and looked at Prenderby. 'This confirms Mr. Chester's story, I think, Mr. Prenderby.'

He turned to the fag again.

'Mr. Chester had been told you were making for top attic.'

'I wasn't, sir, I was making for Beasly's study. When I got there he wasn't in.'

'Did you notice the time?'

'Yes, sir. It was just turned a quarter to

eleven. I looked at the clock, because he'd asked me to bring the stuff over at about eleven, and I remember thinking I was a bit early.'

The Inspector nodded, said: 'Go on, please.'

Montague shuffled nervously. He wondered what punishment he'd get for purveying indecent fiction. That worried him far more than the fact that he was in the middle of a murder investigation.

He continued: 'Beasly came in about eleven. He seemed worried, and in a bit of a temper too. He said old Prend — -er, Mr. Prenderby, had called him to his study to haul him over the coals, and that that had made him late for an appointment he'd had. I showed him the books, and he said he hadn't any money to pay for them at the moment, but he'd see me before he left and settle with me. He said he was going to get the money right away.'

'Did he say from whom?'

'No, sir. I wondered myself. Thought he was borrowing it from one of the chaps.'

'And did you see him again?'

'No, sir. He hadn't put in an appearance by the time I was ready to buzz — leave. So I looked round for him a bit. When I didn't find him, I decided the dirty rotter had sneaked off without paying for the stuff. I went home then.'

Montague was dismissed, and the Inspector looked at Prenderby.

'Do you make anything of that?'

Prenderby frowned. 'Well, I can make quite a lot of it. In the first place, it's obvious Beasly was obtaining money from someone, for some reason. As a possibility, let's say blackmail . . .

'That last morning of term, he had an appointment to see the person in the boxroom. He was after a considerable sum, as witness the fact that he had promised to pay the bookmaker off, and buy the books from Montague.

'Through calling him to my study, he was late for that appointment. After leaving Montague, he hurried off to the top attic to keep the engagement. He found his bird there — but not the bird he'd expected! The worm had turned, to use a time-worn cliché, and in turning had become a viper. Beasly was killed — '

'Wait a minute. How do you know he wasn't strangled somewhere else, then *carried* to the attic?'

'Impracticable,' said Prenderby. 'In a school like this you can't lug bodies about the place — '

'He might have been wrapped in something. Anyone who saw would think it was merely some rubbish being taken to top attic.'

'But it's unlikely, isn't it?'

The inspector said: 'Yes, I suppose it is. Then what we need to know is *who went up to top attic at the time Beasly did.*'

He sent for Brooks again.

'At what time did you go up to top attic, Mr. Brooks?'

Brooks considered for a moment.

'About ten or quarter past.'

'How long were you there?'

'Long enough to throw the bat away.'

'And when you were returning you saw Mr. Chester hurrying to the attic, you say?'

'I did. He was then passing through the

boxroom. It would be about — oh, ten-twenty to ten-thirty, I imagine.'

The inspector pointed to the murder weapon, a dilapidated cricket bat which lay on the table encased in a rubber sheet. He drew the sheet apart.

'This bat, which was used for the purpose of killing Beasly, has the initials H.B.'

Brooks peered at it. Then muttered: 'I'll be damned! It's the bat I threw away!'

'Your bat, Mr. Brooks?'

'Yes, Inspector.'

'Have you any theory as to why your bat was used?'

'Well, since it was the last to be thrown in top attic I expect it was the handiest . . . '

The inspector nodded.

'Thank you. That is all.'

★ ★ ★

The evidence against Frank Chester was beginning to take shape now. He was sent for once more.

'Mr. Chester . . . at what time did you

112

go up to top attic on the last day of term?'

Chester reflected. Then he shook his head slowly.

'I couldn't remember that, Inspector. After ten, I should say.'

'About twenty minutes past?'

'About that.'

'And how long did you remain in top attic?'

'Why, I — half an hour — three quarters — it would be difficult to ascertain the exact period.'

'When you failed to find the books, did you come straight down?'

'Yes.'

'Did you pass anyone on their way up?'

'I — no, I did not.'

The inspector paused a moment, and then: 'Had you any reason for disliking Beasly of North House, Mr. Chester? Were you in the habit of paying him — large sums of money?'

Chester gasped. 'M-money?'

'In short, Mr. Chester, was the boy — blackmailing you, holding something over your head?'

Chester was by no means a tall man.

But he drew himself up to his full height now, some five feet five inches, and said:

'I resent that, Inspector! The suggestion that I would have committed any — indiscretion which would have given a junior schoolboy a hold over me, is outrageous!'

'We are investigating a very serious affair,' said the inspector, gravely.

'Am I to understand that I am under suspicion of having had something to do with this boy's death?'

'Everyone is under suspicion, Mr. Chester.'

'I see. Then I may as well state here and now that I know nothing whatsoever about the matter. Nothing.'

The inspector continued, in a gentler voice. 'It is essential that we endeavour to get at the facts . . . no one is directly accusing you. But it would help — indeed, it is vital you should try to recall the exact time of your departure from top attic. Was it before eleven?'

Chester wilted suddenly and shook his head. 'What's the use, Inspector? I've told you I can't remember. Time has a habit of losing itself when one is rooting through piles of old books.'

'On your way up to the attic, do you remember passing Mr. Brooks, who was on his way down?'

'Yes, I remember that very well indeed.'

The inspector turned away. 'Thank you. That is all for the time being.'

★ ★ ★

Prenderby dropped in to Chester's study in East House that same night. Chester looked up in considerable surprise. He was not used to receiving visits from the master of North House. And at the moment he was in none too rosy a mood. His chin was in his cupped hands, elbows resting on his desk, an open book before him which was wrong-side-up.

Mr. Prenderby dropped into the chair to which Chester motioned him. Chester said: 'Anything wrong?'

Prenderby took from his pocket an envelope. He opened it and drew out the corner of a handkerchief initialled F.C.

'I wondered if this was your property, Chester?'

Chester peered closely.

'Why, yes, that's one of my marked handkerchiefs . . . where did . . . '

'And this?' suggested Prenderby, quickly.

He unfolded his own pocket handkerchief and revealed a cigarette lighter.

Chester looked doubly surprised.

'Where the devil did you get these? That lighter's mine, too. I didn't know I'd lost it until I arrived here for the new term. Where did you find it, Prenderby?'

Prenderby was folding his handkerchief round the lighter again. Chester said: 'Here, I — you might as well leave it, Prenderby. It's *my* lighter.'

Prenderby looked up at him, slowly.

'You say you haven't seen this lighter since last term?'

'That's right. It's an old one I used to keep standing on my desk here. For casual use. I noticed it had gone when I came back this term . . . '

'It hadn't gone before then?'

'Why — I can't say. Might have been missing before the school broke up, if you

116

narrow me down. I was in too much of a rush to notice. Where did you get hold of it?'

Prenderby murmured: 'It was near Beasly's body in the attic. So was your handkerchief!'

Chester went pale, and beads of sweat sprang onto his forehead. His voice was hoarse when he spoke.

'But . . . *Good God!* I — this must make things twice as bad for me — '

Prenderby stood up. He said: 'I'll have to turn these over to the police . . . together with the name of their owner.'

Chester came to his feet, tremblingly. 'Look here, Prenderby, let me have them! I *swear* to you — my word of honour — I know nothing about Beasly's unfortunate end. If you hand things to the police, why, man, it will — '

Prenderby shook his head. 'I'm sorry, Chester. I had meant to cast about for the owner of these items. There are five people in the school with the initials F.C. It was logical to try you first — but I can't withhold them from the police any longer . . . '

117

Chester was panting. He came round the desk rapidly.

'I swear to you — Prenderby, don't turn those over. It — it might — be the means of — *hanging me!* I — '

Prenderby moved away from his imploring hand, He had never liked Chester very much, and this display made him like him even less.

'If you're innocent you have nothing to fear, Chester.'

He moved to the door. Chester's voice came in a despairing cry: 'Prenderby! I *beg* of you — '

Prenderby went out.

★   ★   ★

'Damn it all, don't you realise how serious a thing like withholding evidence can be?' snapped the inspector irritably. 'Why didn't you hand them over before?'

Prenderby shrugged. 'In your hands, everyone would have denied ownership of them, Inspector. In mine — they didn't put two and two together until it was too late.'

The inspector grudgingly admitted that. He said: 'Anyhow, I've had prints taken, and prints of Chester. They match. The only fingerprints on the lighter *are* Chester's.'

Prenderby sighed. 'I was afraid of that.'

'Afraid of it?' questioned the inspector. 'How do you mean?'

Prenderby looked him squarely in the eyes. 'Because I don't for one minute think Chester was the murderer!'

'Why?'

'It fits in too neatly. Everything points to Chester. It's like a film — '

'It's real life,' grunted the police official.

'Then you do think Chester did it?'

'I think so. It seems clear enough. For some reason, Beasly was extorting money from Chester. Chester, faced with a demand for an amount he couldn't hope to raise, decided to kill his tormentor. He went to the boxroom and waited there — lit his cigarette lighter and stood it on some ledge of wood. Beasly was delayed by you, but when he finally came, Chester murdered him. In the struggle the lighter was knocked down, went out — that is how you came to find it with the snuffer lifted and wick burnt out — and Chester, in his fear and excitement, forgot about it. He lost his handkerchief at the same time.'

'Fits in too damned neatly,' muttered Prenderby, shaking his head again. 'If all that is true, why did Chester own up to having been in the boxroom at all?'

'Because if he hadn't, he knew we'd have found out sooner or later. He was seen, remember.'

'What about his reason for coming over to North House?'

'The pornographic books? Just sheer coincidence, and a very lucky alibi for him.'

The North House master looked out of the window across towards East House.

'Are you going to arrest him?'

'What else?'

Abruptly, Prenderby changed the subject.

'Do you think the present killing ties in in any way with the murder of Gregg's daughter in the woods, last term?'

'It would be hard to say. I had noticed there was a similarity. First the strangling, and then the battering of the head to make sure the victim was dead beyond doubt. But that isn't by any means conclusive proof.'

'It seemed to me that there might be a connection,' ventured Prenderby.

'Suppose there was? Suppose the two murders had been committed by the same person?'

'If you could prove they had, it would absolve Chester. You see, Chester was playing chess in the main Masters' Common Room at the time of the previous murder. I know — I was there myself.'

The law shook its head. 'But we can't prove that the two killings are connected, unfortunately, Mr. Prenderby.'

'No, I suppose not. But *I* think they were — and that's why I think Chester is not the man you want! That, and the fact that the whole thing dovetails too neatly to be true.'

8

Mr. Prenderby Sticks to his Guns

Brooks came into Prenderby's classroom looking highly excited. It was the day following the investigation, and nothing very startling had happened either the preceding night or that morning.

But, halfway through the afternoon, Brooks burst in with his bombshell.

Prenderby frowned at him, then nodded towards the class, which had eagerly raised its many heads in avid curiosity.

Brooks grunted: 'It's important, old man. Can you get away for a minute or two?'

Prenderby put the class in the charge of the Head Boy, and went into the corridor.

Brooks was bubbling over with information. The second the door had closed, he said:

'Chester's gone — vanished, just like

Beasly! He didn't turn up to breakfast, if you remember, and he hadn't any classes this morning. I thought maybe he was sleeping in . . . But he didn't turn up to class this afternoon — the Third have gone in with the Science Master again, in East House. I hadn't any class when the inspector arrived, and he asked me to take him to Chester's classroom. I think he was going to arrest him, as you said he would this morning. But when we got there, the class were barging about, and said Chester hadn't turned up. We went to his rooms, but he wasn't there — and his bed hadn't been slept in! His belongings were scattered about the room, as though he'd packed necessities and then got out fast. The inspector was purple with annoyance. He's having the district scoured for him.'

Prenderby snapped: 'The fool!'

'Who — the Inspector?'

'No — Chester! Couldn't he see this will cement the case against him? Running like a scared rabbit.'

'I don't know,' ventured Brooks. 'I fancy I'd be inclined to do a bunk myself, if I had a murder trial facing me. And anyway, what makes you think it wasn't Chester?'

Prenderby shook his head. 'I told you that last night. Chester's actions are not those of a guilty man.'

'But running away — ?'

'As you said yourself, it would be a natural reaction for anyone with Chester's nature. Innocent men have hanged before today. Will again, I expect. But I don't think they could have hanged Chester with what they had. No motive was established, and there were no finger-prints on the bat used to do the injuries to the skull.'

'That's funny,' said Brooks, curiously. 'My *own* fingerprints should have been on that bat. I handled it — '

'It was probably wiped clean after the murder, thereby removing both your prints and those of the killer.'

'But if he had the sense to wipe the bat clean, why didn't he remember the lighter and wipe that?'

'Because he hadn't meant the lighter to be left or found,' pointed out Prenderby.

'In his haste he forgot it. At least, the police think so.'

'You don't?'

'No. It's nothing more than a feeling, mind, Brooks, but I'm sure the lighter — *and* the handkerchief — were left in the boxroom on purpose! Chester was — as the American movies have it — *'framed'.*'

He elucidated still further.

'Are we to believe that a man could use a lighter to light an attic to commit a murder; and then, after being careful enough to wipe prints from the bat, leave said lighter behind — plus a blood-smeared handkerchief? And in any event, the attic is light enough . . . not brilliantly light, but certainly light enough to find a schoolboy's throat and strangle him! Then, after all that, would the man own up to having been in that attic at the time of Beasly's death or thereabouts?'

Brooks looked thoughtful. 'When you put it like that, I see what you mean. Have you mentioned it to the police?'

'I have. But they can only go on evidence, not supposition. The evidence is strong enough to warrant an arrest.'

Brooks lit a cigarette and blew smoke into the frosty air.

'I'm beginning to believe poor old Chester's innocent myself now. But what can we do to clear him?'

'Well, he's made matters worse by running away from the consequences. But, as I see it, the only possible thing we can do now is to find the *real* murderer.'

'That'll be the devil of a job, Prenderby. Nothing like having a shot, though, and I'm with you all along the line. Fact is, I rather fancy myself as a Sherlock Holmes, old man. What can I do to help?'

Prenderby became aware of the growing racket from the form he had just left. He said: 'Nothing; but keep your eyes and ears open, and if you happen on anything which looks as though it would help at all, let me know. We mustn't forget that if Chester is innocent, the murderer is most likely in this school, amongst us every day. Nor must we forget that Beasly was obtaining sums of money from him. All we need is one little clue on which to work, and once we get a lead like that — follow it up until we either prove or disprove Chester's guilt.'

Brooks grinned. 'What a laugh we'd have at the police if we pulled it off.'

Prenderby heard a book thud against the classroom wall. He said: 'I'll have to get back to my little blockheads now. See you later, old man.'

★ ★ ★

Looking towards St. Mark's from the main gates, a casual passer-by would be impressed by the majesty of the School House building, which was under the direct guidance of Dr. Wignall. It was the oldest part of the school — having been built as near as record showed in the year twelve hundred and ninety-two, and subsequently kept in good repair — and housed almost two hundred boys and masters, plus domestic staff.

St. Mark's had been many things in its time. It had started life as a nobleman's castle, and later, in less turbulent times, the moat had been filled in, architectural alterations made, and the castle converted into a monastery.

The order of monks who had had their being behind the walls of St. Mark's had gradually died out. Finally falling on hard times, they had sold the building to a country gentleman, and departed elsewhere to continue their business of becoming extinct in less pretentious surroundings.

Thereafter the place had changed hands many times, until it had finally been purchased as a suitable establishment in which to found a public school. That had been in the year eighteen hundred and thirty, and since then St. Mark's had prospered and grown apace.

In eighteen fifty it had been found necessary to extend the premises, and North House had been built to accommodate the ever-increasing numbers of scholars.

As late as nineteen hundred, a further extension had been called for, and *East* House had sprung up, a comparatively modern red-brick building, which failed to blend in any way with the old grey stones of School House and North House.

The architects had designed North House to match the rest of the school as far as possible, and had succeeded admirably. But when East House had been conjectured, the Board of Governors had decided it would be as well to make it a modern edifice, and overlook the strange contrast between it and its sister houses.

Structurally, of course, School House had also been improved through the ages. The wall which had once surrounded it, and below which had flowed the moat, had vanished entirely, torn down to its foundations. The scar about School House had been hidden by a concrete covering, and now a close search of the quad would not have revealed the fact that centuries ago the School had boasted a moat.

In this proud castle more than a century of youth had had its being, through the dark days — for schoolboys — of the eighteen hundreds, when bullying and beer drinking and brutal masters had been the order of the day, to the more enlightened ages when masters had become almost human, and were becoming more human every passing year.

So School House, with its mellowed stonework and wall slits and twin turrets, stood majestically situated in the precise centre of the quadrangle.

Some one hundred yards to the right, and in a direct line, North House could be seen: smaller than the parent house, and yet with a tradition and beauty all its own, well in keeping with its ancient surroundings

East House, red and squat and ungracious, but nevertheless very comfortable to live in, reared its ugly head on the left of School House, striking an incongruous, jarring note, as outrageous as a saxophone in a symphony orchestra.

The quadrangle behind the houses flared out into a wide semi-circle. At the end of it were the tennis and fives courts, and adjacent to them the small lodge which now served as a school shop. Beyond the courts were the playing fields, utilised for cricket in summer, football in winter.

After these came the woods; the woods where the trees grew thickly, at times excluding light from the dark and narrow paths, where undergrowth grew in tangled masses, and rabbits and squirrels appeared at the appropriate seasons.

The woods were large, and at the opposite side they all but touched Munston Village.

From the main gate of the school, Munston Village was reached by way of a circular road, which added almost three miles to the journey. Anyone desirous of taking a short cut over the fields and through the woods could reach the Village, walking briskly, in about a half hour.

In the old days, the woods had been a time-honoured place for bare-fisted stand-up fights between the St. Mark's boys and the boys of Munston Village. Latterly the enmity had died down, and St. Mark's juniors now settled their own squabbles in the gym, which was attached to the back of East House.

Until last term the woods had still been a favourite haunt of St. Mark's juniors, however. Smoking parties, equipped with packets of cheap cigarettes, would repair thence on hot Saturday and Sunday afternoons and indulge their whims to their hearts' content, far from the prying eyes of masters. At times, junior boys might have been seen meeting seniors on whom they had 'crushes' in the shady recesses of the woods. And, now and again, some plump and pretty village lass with looser morals would meet, by arrangement, a member of the St. Mark's Fifth or Sixth Forms for an interesting evening.

On summer evenings St. Mark's boys were always assured, if they chose to make a pilgrimage to the woods, of finding girls in plenty; girls with buxom bodies and inviting winks and naughty giggles.

For some time it had been in Dr. Wignall's mind to put the woods out of bounds. He had become aware of the growing traffic in sex in the woods between the village belles and the St.

Mark's seniors. But he had hesitated, loath to clamp down a ban on such a long-established landscape feature of St. Mark's. In the prospectus, the words 'backed by pleasant woodlands' *always* appeared. The woods had always been fair territory for generations of St. Mark's boys — it was hard to place them beyond the pale, and unreasonable unless he admitted to *knowing* what went on there.

Then the murder of Gregg's daughter had taken place, and Dr. Wignall had seized upon this as a glorious excuse for putting a very rigid ban on the woods.

St. Mark's juniors rarely went there now. The punishment offered to anyone found breaking bounds was too great, consisting as it did of detention for six consecutive half-holidays. But the seniors still patronised the woods and the local damsels, and had so far been lucky in attracting no official interference. The masters suspected, but the seniors were far too careful to be seen heading in the direction of what was now forbidden territory.

The woods had attractions other than

girls. On the west side, on the main Branshoot road, nestled a little ivy-clad pub known locally as the 'Swill Bin', although the name above the door said, 'Scarlet Rabbit'.

The proprietor, at some risk to himself, catered for the senior St. Mark's students. Here they could indulge in a quiet game of cards or snooker, and several glasses of good English ale. That the charges were high, they cared little. They felt the landlord should rightly be indemnified for the risk he took in ministering to their needs; were the fact that he not only sold them beer and liquor, but also on occasion, let to some senior and maid the tiny room at the rear of the place for an afternoon or evening — were *this* fact to come to light, he would not only lose his license, but probably receive a term of imprisonment for keeping a disorderly house.

The masters very seldom visited the Swill Bin. They preferred the more modern atmosphere of the roadhouse, a recent innovation standing about six hundred yards from St. Mark's on the main road.

On Friday nights the roadhouse ran a dance, and this was always well-attended by the masters of St. Mark's and Morefell College, and the younger mistresses of Munston Girls' School. Pleasant friendships were formed, and mutual problems discussed.

Seniors of St. Mark's were permitted to attend this dance, as were the older girls of Munston Girls' School. There was no drinking in the dance hall itself, and both Dr. Wignall and his feminine counterpart at Munston Girls' foresaw no lasting harm in this mingling of the sexes, which was well-chaperoned by both the masters and mistresses of the respective schools.

They were unaware that friendships begun in the roadhouse were all too often cemented very immorally in the *Swill Bin*!

It was here that Baxter, popular and suntanned Sixth Former, had made the acquaintance of the delightful Miss Payne.

Baxter was nineteen, keen and ambitious, a good swimmer and a great sportsman. Rumour had it that he would one day play for his country on the cricket fields. He had already played for the county, and made an admirable showing.

Marjorie Payne of Munston Girls' was in her eighteenth year, was lusciously formed (so that despite her somewhat severe school uniform she attracted the attention of many males who should have known better), was a keen supporter of sport in all its forms, and an excellent swimmer.

Baxter and she had danced together at the roadhouse, and had found so much in common — particularly swimming — that they had arranged for a late-night swim in the nearby river. This was last term, before the murder had taken place.

The swim had gone off very well, once Baxter had recovered from his embarrassment at seeing a young lady unashamedly in the nude.

For Marjorie, quite a sweet girl on the face of it, knew her way round.

'I think it's so silly, this taboo against being natural,' she told him, complacently slipping out of her dress. 'I don't know about *you*, but *I* hate anything clinging to me when I'm swimming. I like to swim *free* — '

Baxter felt uncomfortable, and fumbled with his bathing trunks. He wasn't quite prepared for this kind of business, as he put it to himself.

'I used to be quite *prudish* myself,' said Marjorie, noting his embarrassment. 'But when I was on holiday in London last year, I was invited to a private nudist party for the weekend at Elstree. Once I got *used* to the idea, I wasn't embarrassed at all. It's only fools and deformed persons who're ashamed of nakedness.'

Faced by that remark, Baxter stoutly laid aside his trunks and joined her in a sportive romp in the water.

As Marjorie had known, it had its inevitable conclusion, and thereafter their meetings had been frequent and passionate.

The landlord of the Swill Bin found them good customers. It was their practice to break bounds after midnight at least once a month, and stay together in his little back room for two or three hours.

One night, about a week after the unfortunate Frank Chester had bolted with the myrmidons of the law hot upon his trail, Marjorie lay awake in her narrow bed at Munston Girls' School.

About her, the healthy breathing of her companions filled the shadowy dormitory, and an occasional snore woke the echoes.

Nearby the clock in Munston church struck the midnight hour. Marjorie rose silently, fumbled in her locker.

Here she had clothes purchased in the West End on her last vacation. Silk, fully-fashioned stockings; frothy step-ins; a quite unnecessary pair of brassieres which she felt made her more of a woman; neat tan-and-white shoes; an expensive perfume; a sophisticated dark brown costume; a chic little hat and gloves to match.

All this for the benefit of Baxter, who was proving a considerable antidote to the utter boredom she experienced during school term.

She dressed quickly, and was adjusting her tiny hat when a cautious voice from the next bed muttered: 'Marge. Is that *you?*'

'Go to sleep, Phyllis,' she hissed in annoyance. 'Want to wake the whole darned dorm up?'

'But Marge, you aren't going *out*, surely?'

'Of course I am. Think I'm dressed just for the fun of it?'

'To — to the Swill Bin again?'

'Yes — Eric's meeting me there.'

Phyllis was her choice of friend, and they held nothing from each other. Phyllis was the daughter of a Bishop, and her early upbringing caused her to be horrified at the nocturnal activities of her friend. She had resisted all suggestions made by Marjorie that she should 'see a bit of life'. She never allowed herself to meet any boys, or to listen to Marjorie's somewhat vulgar anecdotes. Apart from this, though, she had a warm regard for the faster girl, and valued the friendship. It was a case of opposites attracting. There was nothing in the nature of a schoolgirl 'crush' about the affair; it was a firm and sincere friendship. Marjorie had come to respect her friend's nature; and Phyllis to tolerate, if not condone, Marjorie's immorality.

Ordinarily she never protested these midnight ramblings of Marjorie's. But this time it was different.

'But Marge, you're not going — through the woods, are you?'

'Naturally I am, Phyll. Why not?'

Phyllis shivered. 'You know what happened to that Gregg girl. And — '

Marjorie laughed lightly. 'That was a long time ago, darling. I'm not afraid of anything like that ... might even *welcome* it,' she added, 'providing he didn't murder me afterwards,' and had the satisfaction of chuckling at Phyllis' shocked gasp.

'Don't clown, Marge. I know the murder happened a long time ago, but — well, some people are saying that the man who killed the Gregg girl was the one who murdered that St. Mark's boy. And he's still at large — the police haven't caught him yet.'

'He isn't in this district, anyhow. They're sure of that.'

'How can they be *sure* when they don't know where he is?'

'Oh, phooey,' said Marjorie, carelessly. 'Probably no connection between the murders. And anyhow, I won't bump into him. Do go to sleep, Phyll, there's a darling. Unless — you want to come along with me?'

Phyllis shuddered: 'You know I don't. But do be careful, Marge.'

'Eric and I are always *very* careful, darling,' said Marjorie, deliberately mis-understanding. 'After all, I haven't any desire to be turfed out of Munston into the cold, cold snow, clutching a little bundle wrapped in a shawl in my arms. God forbid!'

Then she was out of the dormitory and creeping downstairs to the servants' entrance at the back. She had a key to this door, purchased from one of the maids, long since dismissed. She could let herself out and in at any time, since there were no bolts.

Hugging the shadows, she sneaked

round the rear of the school to the tradesmen's entrance. She emerged into the road, cut across, climbed the stile, and ploughed her way over a field of stubble, taking care to avoid scratching her stockings.

The woods loomed large and black before her, and without any trace of nerves she entered them.

At times it was pitch dark, the full moon rays cut off by the arch of branches above; tangled, knotty branches. But she knew her way too well to hesitate. She followed the winding path.

The moon suddenly lost itself behind a black patch of cloud, and only a meagre starlight illuminated her course. And it was at that moment she heard a crackling of twigs as someone stepped into the path behind her!

9

Mr. Gregg Wanders Nocturnally

Marjorie's first reaction was one of sheer terror. But, being a level-headed girl, she quickly conquered this. Though her heart pounded sickeningly, she clenched her fists and looked about for something with which to defend herself.

She had stopped walking, and half-turned to face her follower. Now she could discern a dark shadow beneath one of the trees which lined the narrow path.

The moon swam into the sky from behind the patch of cloud, and the man standing there was revealed to her in the pallid white light which shone down through the crooked branches.

She recognised him at once. She had seen him many times at the dance at the roadhouse. He was a master from St. Mark's: the one who had — lost his daughter in these same woods. The father of the girl who had been murdered last term!

She sought for his name — of course, Gregg!

He spoke suddenly.

'I hope I didn't startle you?'

'I — you — '

'I see I did. I'm sorry, I heard you moving in the darkness, and for one instant I thought — ' He paused, and she noticed the peculiar, staring expression in his eyes. She felt afraid again, suddenly.

'What are you doing in the woods at this time of night?' he demanded, stepping closer.

She thought she might very well have asked the same question of him.

'Just — just walking,' she told him, evasively.

He grunted. 'Haven't you more sense than to go through this place after midnight? Or any time, for that matter? Don't you know there's a — murderer at large?'

'I — no,' she told him, feeling it would be an answer open to less argument.

He was surprised. 'You don't? Then

you aren't one of the village girls?'

She lied: 'No, I'm a stranger here. Staying with friends.'

He looked at her keenly, and she thanked Heaven she hadn't got on her school uniform. At length, he murmured, 'Then your friends should have warned you about the woods. They aren't very healthy for young girls — for any girls — to be walking in. There was a girl — killed here some months ago. The police believe the murderer is still at large. I believe that myself, too — '

He became aware of her expression of alarm, and laughed without mirth. 'I see what you're thinking. You think, being a stranger here, that possibly *I* am the killer? I can assure you I'm not. As a matter of fact, I'm looking for him myself . . . I have — reason to. And if I find him — '

He left the words unfinished, but his expression sent a shiver down her spine.

She had to keep up the pretext of being a stranger. She said:

'Are you a detective, then?'

He shook his head. 'Nothing like that.

145

Just a schoolmaster. But I think perhaps I had better escort you back to your friends' home . . . it isn't safe for you here.'

'Oh, no, thank you,' she told him quickly. 'I'll go right home now. I'll be all right.'

He looked dubious. 'No, young lady. I think I'll be your escort this time. I wouldn't like anything to happen to you. As it happened to my — '

He stopped speaking abruptly, and moved towards her.

'You needn't be afraid of me. Just keep close behind me and I'll see you safe. Exactly where are you staying?'

After a moment's thought, she replied: 'Close to the Scarlet Rabbit. Do you know it?'

'The public house? Yes, of course.'

He started moving, and she walked after him. She hoped that they wouldn't bump into Baxter. If they did, it would be too bad for Baxter.

They didn't. They reached the Scarlet Rabbit without incident, and here he turned to face her. 'Now where?'

146

'I can find my way from here, thank you. It's just along the road.'

'I had better come with you.'

'Please, no. If my friends happened to see me with a man at this hour, they'd — they'd think all kinds of wrong things. It's been very good of you to take me home, but I can manage from here. Thank you.'

'Very well. But allow me to *warn* you, young lady — don't venture into these woods again after dark. Things lurk in the shadows — unpleasant incidents can happen — ask your friends to tell you about it . . . Remember what I say — '

His eyes frightened her again. They were so strange. She felt the death of his daughter must have left him slightly off normal.

Without speaking again, he turned and strode back along the path. He moved quietly, stealthily, as if he hoped to take someone or something by surprise.

Marjorie shuddered and felt cold suddenly. She didn't, after all, feel much like keeping that date with Baxter now. But she shrugged off her unpleasant feelings, and pushed open the back gate of the Scarlet Rabbit.

There was a dim light burning behind the drawn curtains of a room on the right. That showed Eric had arrived. She tapped on the door with relief, and the landlord admitted her.

'Your young man's in there,' he told her, with a wink to which she took no exception. 'Lucky young devil, eh?'

She tickled him under the chin. 'Nice to know you think so, Joey darling. Shall I go in?'

He gave her a leer. 'Unless you'd rather come and share *my* bed?'

She laughed, and he added: 'I reckon that's a bit too much for an old cove like me to hope for, eh? Any'ow, don't you two young rips forget to switch off the lights and slam the door until the latch catches when you leave. I'm off to roost now. Night.'

'Good night, Joey dear.'

He went upstairs, and she opened the door of the room on her right and went inside.

The room was in darkness except for

the flickering firelight, which she had spotted through the drawn curtains. Baxter uncoiled his length from the settee in front of the fire when she came in, and greeted her with enthusiasm.

'Marge, darling. Thought you were never coming.'

She flung her arms round him and they strained to each other, tightly. Her lips brushed his as she murmured: 'Eric, my little lamb, you and I don't see half enough of each other. My God, you have no *idea* how that damned school and those half-baked kids that infest it bore me. It isn't life — just insincerity. It's all a sham, all wrong — *this* is life . . . the only kind of life that matters.'

Baxter demurred. 'I don't know about that, Marge. I like *my* school. Think a hell of a lot of St. Mark's, and everything that goes with it. Besides — we'd never have met if the schools hadn't brought us together, would we?'

'No,' she admitted. 'But there'd have been some other girl for you — and some other *men*, for me.'

'Marjorie!' he expostulated. 'You don't

mean that? You know why we do what we do — it isn't like those clandestine meetings some of the chaps have with the village girls. Damn it all, I'm in *love* with you — and you with me. Aren't you?'

She felt he had to be solaced. She pressed her moist, open mouth to his, and murmured: 'Of course I am, darling. You mustn't mind what I say. I'm only joking. You don't think I'd be like this with anyone else, do you — surely?'

Baxter told himself he didn't. He had to tell himself hard.

Marjorie thought: The bloody noble fool. Full of highfalutin ideas to justify his messing me about. God, he might even get round to asking me to *marry* him — he's the type!

But for all that, she loved Baxter — at the moment. He was tall and handsome, and fast becoming experienced under her able tuition. Marjorie was a good tutor — she was a hungry woman.

She said, when they had broken the clinch and gone to ground on the settee, 'Darling, pour me something out. What did he leave for us?'

150

'Beer and wine.'

'Make it beer,' she told him. 'I've always held the view that wine dulls the emotions, and that would be too dreadful.'

He handed her a glass and she drank thoughtfully. He poured himself a beer and joined her.

'You were late tonight.'

She lit a cigarette and nodded. Offered them to Baxter.

'Thanks, no. Have to keep fit — running in a cross-country race tomorrow. I'm with the hares . . .'

She laughed uncontrollably. 'Sweet, you *are* funny. You refuse a cigarette and accept a night with me! Believe me, Eric, the night will do far more to ruin your chances than the fag will. Take it.'

'You're right, of course. I shouldn't have come.'

She looked at him through her eyelashes.

'Shouldn't you? Could you have stayed away so easily, then?'

He grinned, somewhat ruefully. 'Marge, it wouldn't make any difference if my life depended on that blasted run. I'd have had to come tonight.'

She nestled closer to him.

★   ★   ★

'Oh, I almost forgot,' she said later, when they were lying back on the settee. 'The reason I was late tonight was because I bumped into someone in the woods . . . '

Baxter jumped. 'You *what?* Who?'

She stroked his brow soothingly. 'Eric, you needn't get alarmed. I didn't get raped. At least, not until I got here. I bumped into one of the masters from your coll . . . that Gregg man.'

'Gregg? Good Lord, what the devil was *Gregg* doing in the woods at an hour like this?'

'He looked strange,' she told him. 'And from what I was able to gather, he was looking for the person who murdered his daughter last term . . . the old trout gave me quite a lecture on the evils of walking alone in the woods at night.'

Baxter said, uneasily: 'Didn't recognise you, did he?'

152

'Heavens, what would a master be doing recognising a poor little schoolgirl like myself? He doesn't even know me, and fortunately I was wearing ordinary clothes, so he hadn't any idea I was from Munston Girls'.'

Baxter breathed again, thankfully.

'I shall have to be bloody careful going back,' he told her. 'If old Gregg were to see *me* — I shudder to think what it might mean. Most likely the sack.'

She asked curiously: 'Does he often prowl about at night?'

'I've heard rumours to that effect. He's — queer. Though he does his work well enough, and it isn't anything you could lay a finger on.'

'But would your Head allow a master to wander as Gregg does?'

'I suppose he wouldn't, if he knew.'

She smiled. 'He warned me to stay out of the woods at night.'

'Are you going to?'

'Of course not. We'll meet just as usual, Eric. I wouldn't stay away from you if King Kong himself were charging about in the vicinity . . . '

'Just the same, I think you'd better let me come for you in future . . . wait by your school wall until I get there. Then we can go to the Swill Bin together.'

She shook her head. 'No, Eric. Makes it doubly risky. Let's stick to the present arrangement.'

He argued for some time, but she finally convinced him. And they agreed to meet again the following month as usual.

'That Mr. Gregg may have stopped prowling by then,' she said, stretching luxuriously. 'If he hasn't, for Heaven's sake watch out, Eric. I don't know what I'd do to occupy myself if I didn't have our meetings to look forward to each month.'

Eric grunted and ran his hand through her hair. 'May be more than just Gregg barging through the woods,' he told her. 'I hear Prenderby's taking a hand in this case —'

'Prenderby?'

'He's master of North House. A nice chap — best master at St. Mark's. You know, *human*. I mean he's the type of man who, if he caught us here together, would do his duty, but do it without looking on us as if we were a couple of naughty kids. He'd understand.'

She stared into the fire with parted lips.

'Sounds interesting. Is he the tall man I've seen at the dance once or twice — smokes a pipe and looks awfully like Leslie Howard?'

'That's Prenderby,' admitted Eric Baxter.

'Hmm. I'd like to meet him sometime. I expect he'd be fascinating company.'

For some reason, Baxter felt himself growing jealous. He snorted and changed the subject.

'It's getting on for three — we'd better be getting back again, hadn't we?'

She sighed and began to arrange her clothing. They had a final drink, switched on the light whilst Marjorie combed her hair before the mantelpiece mirror, and then left the room.

Baxter closed the back door of the pub, and made sure the latch was on.

'I'd better come as far as the school wall with you,' he pleaded.

'Well — ' She was anxious not to leave him for a while yet. 'All right, Eric. It will

155

be risky. But — we'll chance it.'

They began to walk . . . and as they drew nearer to Munston Girls' School, they grew a little less cautious. So they were entirely unaware of the shadow which glided along behind them until Baxter, dropping his hat, stooped to pick it up . . .

The next second he shouted: 'Hell's bells! *Run* — '

They ran together, his hand gripping her arm and jerking her along with him wildly through the undergrowth. A shout rang through the still air after them.

'You young scoundrel — *stop*! Do you *hear?*'

They heard, but refused to heed. Not until they were deep in a clump of weeds, and far from danger, did they stop.

Marjorie panted, and clung to him for support.

'What *was* it, Eric? *Who* was it?'

'Gregg again,' he cursed. 'I spotted him when I bent down to pick up my lid. Prowling behind us.'

She caught her breath sharply. 'Do — do you think he knew you?'

Baxter shook his head. 'I think, if he'd recognised me, he'd have shouted to me by name. But I do think he saw I was wearing a school blazer and cap — damn the luck. This has properly pranged everything now.'

They continued the return journey to Marjorie's school more cautiously thereafter.

At the wall, in the shadows, Baxter stopped and took her into his arms.

'This means there might be a hue and cry at St. Mark's. Luckily Gregg'll think you're one of the village lasses. Of course, on the other hand he may not wish to draw attention to the fact that he prowls the woods all night, and may say nothing at all about having seen a St. Mark's senior there. But for the time being we have to play our cards carefully. Don't do anything, darling, until you hear from me. Better not even see one another for a few days or so . . . until I'm sure everything's all right.'

'But Eric, how will I know when to meet you again?'

He thought a moment, then: 'If we

don't happen to see each other about, I'll get a note to you. But until we know how we stand, don't even come near me. If I was bowled out — and Gregg can be a sly customer, you know, may have recognised me and say nothing about it just so's he can find out *which* girl I'm so interested in — as I say, if I was bowled out, it would be a nasty thing for you to be implicated in. Best thing is to stay right away from me until we're sure. Don't even speak to me at the dances on Fridays until everything's back to normal. Tell you what, though — you can send Phyllis over to see if I've anything to report. When the coast's clear I'll bung along a note by her.'

Marjorie laughed lightly. 'All right. I'll hate it, but I'll do it, Eric. One thing — for Heaven's sake, don't let Phyll know what's *in* the note. She'd throw a fit if she fancied she was carrying notes arranging rendezvous for us. She'd feel sure the eternal fires were going to be her allotted portion.'

She kissed him passionately, clung to him. Then he waited until she had opened the gate and entered the school premises. Her voice drifted back over the wall in a whisper: 'Night, dear.'

Baxter turned. Despite the meeting with Gregg he was feeling on top of everything. He always felt like that after an evening with Marjorie. He was really very deeply in love with her, and too stubborn to allow himself to believe that she was not worthy of a deep and sincere love.

He cut round the outskirts of the woods, feeling that Gregg would confine his ramblings to the more heavily-wooded areas.

What the deuce did Gregg hope to gain by wandering about like that? Baxter asked himself. The man must be crazy.

He reached St. Mark's without further hindrance, and was soon climbing through the side scullery window. From there it was just a step to his own study with its bed in an alcove.

He undressed and got between the sheets with pleasant thoughts of Marjorie doing the same. He wished that she had been there beside him. But better not to see her for a few weeks — until he was *sure* Gregg hadn't any idea of the identity of the St. Mark's senior whom he had encountered in the woods with a girl. Yes, he thought drowsily, take it easy —

Outside, in the woods, Gregg *still* wandered . . .

10

Mr. Prenderby is Merciful

Each of the houses at St. Mark's had its own Masters' Common Room. School House Common Room, however, was usually the central gathering point for the three assortments of teachers. It was large and well-decorated, and here masters gathered after the day's work was done, if they felt inclined, for a chat about school affairs.

It was to the Main Common Room that Prenderby and Brooks repaired, the night after the incident in the woods. As yet, they were no nearer to a solution of the mystery which they felt still surrounded Beasly and his untimely death; but Prenderby was still hopeful, and Brooks was still keeping eyes and ears open.

They were discussing the paper chase of that morning with Markham, Fifth

Form Master of School House.

'I thought it would have been a walkover for Baxter of your house,' said Markham, a thin, stooped man with pince-nez and a friendless soul. 'I believe he didn't even finish the run.'

Prenderby frowned and puffed vigorously at his pipe.

'Can't make it out,' he announced after a moment. 'Baxter was on top of his form yesterday at the trial. He outdistanced every other runner — and I'd have sworn he had the staying power.'

Brooks hazarded: 'The kid looked absolutely played out when he toed the line this morning. *I* fancied he'd have had the hounds beaten silly. Not like him to lie down on a job. But when I saw him this morning, I'd have bet right away that they'd nab him long before the halfway mark was reached.'

'And so they did,' nodded Prenderby. 'Collapsed, I believe. Makes me wonder if he'd been smoking a bit much lately — '

'Smoking never caused those circles under his eyes,' Brooks countered.

Markham pursed his lips. 'Of course,

boys of his age often cling to bad habits, Prenderby . . . if you see what I mean?'

'I think I do. And I don't credit Baxter — or should I say, discredit him — with any of those tricks. He's a sensible lad.'

Markhan shrugged and moved away to speak to Collins of East. Gregg, who had been standing alone in one corner of the room, eyeing the group of three, moved over immediately.

'Hello, Prenderby — Brooks.'

'Evening, Gregg.'

Gregg glanced round. 'I've been wanting a word with you, Prenderby. Waited until Markham sheered off. It's a matter concerning your house, I think. No need to let the school in on it.'

Prenderby tapped out his pipe on the side of the fireplace and said, 'Go on, Gregg, I'm all ears.'

Gregg seemed to have some slight difficulty in making a start, then: 'Last night, I happened to be in the woods — '

Brooks opened his mouth to say something and was silenced by a quick glance from his senior master. Prenderby had too much sense to begin asking Gregg what he had been doing there.

Gregg went on. 'It was after midnight, and I bumped into a young woman, alone, making her way down the centre path. I told her how risky it was for her there, and offered to see her home. She accepted the offer, and I took her safely as far as the Scarlet Rabbit.'

He paused again, and Brooks blurted out, 'But what has all that to do with our house?'

Gregg grunted. 'I'm coming to that. Well, this girl told me she was staying with friends, and would go straight to them there and then.

'It must have been almost three hours later that, as I was returning to the school myself, I came out on a path behind a boy, and the girl I'd spoken to previously.

'I followed them for a minute or two, trying to identify the boy — he was a St. Mark's senior, I knew by his clothing. Then he dropped his cap, bent to retrieve it, and spotted me. He ran, of course, and ignored my shouts for him to come back . . . '

Prenderby murmured, 'Why are you telling me this?'

'He was from your house, Prenderby. I saw the initial N on his blazer pocket when he bent down . . . '

Prenderby nodded. The houses at St. Mark's distinguished their inmates by means of initials emblazoned on the blazer pocket: S for School House, E for East, N for North.

Brooks said: 'Of course, it may have been a boy from another house wearing a North House blazer.'

Prenderby shook his head. 'That's unlikely, Brooks. Did you recognise this senior, Gregg?'

Gregg made a gesture of negation. 'No, I couldn't swear to the boy's identity — but it looked like Baxter, the senior from your house. Sixth Form, isn't he?'

'Yes, yes . . . and you say he was with a *girl?*'

'The girl to whom I had spoken earlier.'

'A local girl?'

'She told me she was a stranger, but doubtless she was lying.'

Prenderby looked at Brooks, then

asked, 'Have you reported this matter to the Headmaster, Mr. Gregg?'

'Of course not, I don't wish to — to draw attention to my own — er — movements. Dr. Wignall would not understand — but you do, do you not, Mr. Prenderby? I can't rest — you can appreciate how I feel? I have a premonition that the woods will eventually disgorge the — murderer — I — '

Prenderby patted his arm.

'All right, Gregg.'

'I thought you should know about the senior. At first, I had decided to keep the whole thing to myself and thus avoid drawing attention to my actions. But when I thought it over, I decided that it was my duty to at least inform you of what I had seen. Should there be any trouble connected with this senior breaking bounds and consorting with women — probably loose — in the woods, you would be in an unenviable position, Prenderby. Now that you know, even if you can do nothing more, you *can* take steps to ascertain who it was I saw, and put a stop to his illicit meetings, which may be quite a regular thing.'

Prenderby lit his pipe again. 'Thank you, Gregg. I shall most certainly look into the matter. It was good of you to mention it to me.'

Gregg nodded. 'As to myself, I would prefer it, should you speak of the affair to the Headmaster, if you could endeavour to keep my own name out of the discussion.'

'I will not be mentioning it to Dr. Wignall,' Prenderby told him. 'First I will go into it thoroughly, and if Baxter admits to being the culprit, I will warn him not to engage in similar escapades again.'

Gregg said: 'I think that should meet the case, as the circumstances are so peculiar. Good night, Prenderby.'

They said good nights, and Gregg went out. Brooks looked at his senior master.

'You mean if you find out that Baxter did break bounds to meet some girl, you'll let him off scot-free?'

'This time, yes.'

'But, good God, Prenderby, if the Head knew — '

'The Head will not know,' said

Prenderby, 'for who is to inform him? Surely not Baxter himself, if he is guilty? And most certainly not Gregg.'

'But breaking bounds after midnight — and meeting with a tart . . . that was what she must have been, or the equivalent. You should punish him for that.'

'Possibly. But I shall overlook it this time, as I said. You must remember Baxter's age — '

'He's only a schoolboy.'

'A young man,' corrected Prenderby. 'Turned nineteen. And with all the desires inherent in a normal young male of his age. I wouldn't justify his actions, but I certainly won't condemn them.'

'You'll *condone* them?'

Prenderby shrugged. 'It isn't a question of what he and the girl have been doing at all. We have to look at this thing from the angle of the reputation of the school, and the duty I owe to it and Dr. Wignall. I am getting paid for doing a job, Brooks, and I intend to do it as well as I may. Damn it, man, I don't *blame* Baxter, if it was he. Will you try to tell me you yourself never

168

did anything like that, Brooks?'

'I certainly did not — at *his* age,' said Brooks, indignantly.

'Nor would have, had the opportunity presented itself?' said Prenderby with a slight smile.

Brooks flushed, then grinned. 'If I am to answer that question honestly, I must answer yes,' he said.

'Of course you must,' Prenderby agreed. 'Brooks, I knew my first woman when I was seventeen years old, and even then considered I'd waited quite an unreasonable length of time for that privilege. She was a girl from the local tobacconist's shop in the village near my home. I still think of her with a rather wistful feeling . . . she was a sweet kid, about my own age. God knows what became of her.'

Brooks was used to these confidences. Prenderby was, and had always been, outspoken. His life was by no means blameless, but he made no effort to conceal the fact.

Prenderby continued, 'So, who am I to say to Baxter or anyone else, 'Thou Shalt

Not' — thou shalt not seduce a woman? All I can say is, 'For the Lord's sake, boy, think of the *school*, and of the mess I'd get into if it was found out.' Then leave it up to his conscience.'

'Of which schoolboys have very little,' ventured Brooks.

'You're wrong there. The public school system may have its faults, and a devil of a lot of them, but one thing it does breed is a strong sense of honour and responsibility. I'm speaking now of the normal boy. There are exceptions to every rule, naturally. But Baxter's a normal boy. I don't think he'll resent my putting it to him that way, assuming he was seen and Gregg was not suffering from hallucinations.'

'That's a strong possibility, now you mention on it,'

'But just a possibility. While Gregg is very far from being his normal merry self, I still contend that he is well in control of his mind. Besides, I'm not entirely surprised by this affair. I fancy I know where Baxter and the girl had been until that hour.'

Brooks jumped. 'You think they'd been somewhere?'

'The Scarlet Rabbit. Or, if you prefer the local name — Swill Bin.'

'But it was after midnight. The place would have been closed — '

'That wouldn't have made any difference. You see, poor old Chester was quite friendly with the proprietor of the place. Though the man never mentioned it to him, Chester was convinced that he kept a back room especially for St. Mark's seniors and their lady loves of the moment. It all sounds pretty revolting, but Chester says that he once spotted a St. Mark's senior leaving the room with a village girl, late at night. The pub proprietor steered him out of the way quickly, of course ... Chester was uncertain what to do, but since he was friendly with the man he decided to ignore it and pretend he hadn't seen anything. There wasn't any great bond between Chester and myself, but apparently — according to his *own* statement — he considered me the only master at St. Mark's to whom he could make a confidence of that nature with a certainty of its being *kept* a confidence. He put the whole thing to me and asked me what I thought he should do. He mentioned that he had an idea that that back room was used regularly by seniors. I told him it was his duty to make the matter known to Dr. Wignall, or at least to warn his friend off. I don't know what course he took, if he took any, but I heard nothing more about the pub-crawlers.'

Brooks gasped. 'You kept it to yourself?'

'It was a confidence, remember? I wouldn't be telling except that I know you're quite able to keep a secret yourself.'

Soon afterwards, he left Brooks and ambled back to North House. He made his way to the Sixth Form passage, to Baxter's study. He didn't wish to interview Baxter in his own rooms. He wanted to make the chat they were to have as informal, as man-to-man, as possible.

He tapped and Baxter said: 'Come in.'

Baxter was sitting in front of a dying fire, his elbows on his knees and his chin

172

on his hands. As Prenderby entered, he grunted:

'What is it?'

'I thought you'd be able to spare a few minutes for a chat,' said Prenderby, genially, and Baxter jumped as he recognised his master's voice.

'Oh — oh, it's *you*, sir. I didn't know. Thought it was some ass come to jaw about — sit down, sir.'

Prenderby closed the door and made himself comfortable in an armchair. Baxter looked at him curiously.

'Sorry I made such a mucker of the chase today, sir. It would have been a feather in the House cap if I'd pulled it off. Fact is, I wasn't feeling up to scratch.'

'The chase doesn't matter a great deal, Baxter — but you could hardly expect to feel on form after a night spent roaming round the woods, could you?'

Baxter's mouth fell open. He gulped. 'Then Gregg — I mean, Mr. Gregg — he — '

'Before you say anything more, Baxter, Mr. Gregg is not certain whom he saw. He *thinks* it might have been you. Was it?'

For one moment, Baxter looked as if he was gathering himself for a flat denial. Then: 'It — *might* have been, sir.'

'I see. May I ask what you were doing there, Baxter?'

Baxter was a clam.

Prenderby repeated, 'I see. The age of chivalry is *not* dead. There was a lady in the case.'

It was a statement, not a question. Baxter said: 'Yes, sir.'

Prenderby leaned forward. 'You know what this *means*?'

Baxter mumbled, miserably, 'The sack, I expect. I'll be turfed out of the school.'

'You would be — if Dr. Wignall was aware of your conduct. But it would mean much more than that. It would mean an investigation — which would probably result in revealing where you'd spent your leisure with the lady in question. That would mean, in its turn, a court case — and a dreadful scandal for the school!'

Baxter looked at him forlornly. 'Then you know where we'd been? You know about the — '

Prenderby silenced him with a gesture.

'I have an idea. And I have no desire to know any more. But can you see what you are risking by these midnight meetings? Your own expulsion, the revelation of the identity of the girl you consort with, and the ruination of the name of your school! Food for much thought there, Baxter. Is it *worth it*, man?'

Baxter hung his head.

Prenderby went on, 'I take it these nocturnal rendezvous have a certain regularity?'

'I've met — the girl more than once, yes sir.'

'And you'll give me your word that they will now *cease*?'

Baxter started, looked up with a new hope in his eyes.

'You — you mean you're not — not going to report this to the — to Dr. Wignall, sir?'

'I have already decided that,' said Prenderby, leaning back again. 'I want your word, Baxter — and then the entire thing will be forgotten. Will you give it?'

'But gosh, sir — hell — I mean, er — yes. Gladly.'

Prenderby stood up.

'Baxter, I *should* report this. I should have that idiot at the Scarlet Rabbit arrested and you expelled — but sometimes it happens that concealment will do less harm than exposure. If this came out, the name of St. Mark's would stink for the length and breadth of England. People would assume such things must happen at every public school. It is a matter that could not be hushed up, coming as it does after the recent murder, and the escape of Mr. Chester. Therefore, Baxter, as long as you give your word that you will not visit this place of rendezvous again with this girl, I will overlook the whole thing.'

Baxter said, steadily: 'You have my word, sir.'

Prenderby nodded. 'By the way, I want you to tell the same thing to any other of the seniors whom you know are in the habit of going to the same place. I think that is all . . . good night, Baxter.'

'Good night, sir — and thank you. I'd hate to he pitched out of the school, and hate still more to be the cause of having the school's good name dragged through the slime.'

'Then remember that when next you are tempted to forget your word of honour,' Prenderby said, smiling.

Then the door closed behind him, and Baxter sat staring for quite a long time; thankful, deeply thankful, that it was possible for masters like old Prenderby to exist, and more still that it hadn't been one of the others who'd caught him out. Whatever anyone might think, Prenderby was being merciful sitting on the denouement. Merciful not only to Baxter, but to St. Mark's. Nor had Baxter been made to feel cheap or dirty or small. He was grateful for that, too. It wasn't a question of stopping his immoral conduct. Just one of thinking of the school. That way it *sounded* better. It would be hard to give up Marjorie — but it was one of those things that had to be done!

11

Mr. Lodge Receives an
Unpleasant Surprise

The C.I.D. man from Branshoot flicked ash from his cigar and crossed one elegant leg above the other.

'We haven't been hovering round during the past two weeks to no purpose, Mr. Prenderby,' he said, with a slightly superior air. 'I understand you have been interesting yourself in the case . . . ?'

Prenderby drew vigorously at his pipe and flicked the match from the open window.

'I have, Inspector.'

'I heard. That's why I dropped in here. To tell you that you needn't bother from here on. The whole thing is pretty well sewn up . . .'

Prenderby raised puzzled brows. 'You haven't got hold of Chester yet, have you?'

'We will in time. We're certain he hasn't left the country, and it's just a question of patience until he falls into our little net.'

'Then in what way have you got the case sewn up?'

The Inspector leaned forward and stressed the point with his glowing cigar.

'Motive, Mr. Prenderby! We have discovered a perfect motive for the crime which implicates Chester.'

Prenderby was intrigued. He said, 'Don't stop now, Inspector. Or am I not supposed to know?'

'No reason that you shouldn't,' the inspector told him, smiling. 'Matter of fact, it came out during a careful questioning of the junior schoolboys. The Second and Third Form boys. One of these — *Carfax*, I think, is his name — admitted to one of our men that Chester *had* something to hide. It appeared Chester was homosexually inclined, Prenderby. Did you know about that?'

Prenderby shook his head. 'I did not. Chester always seemed to be very quiet and a good master. If he was lacking in any one thing, it was in not having as firm control as he might have had over his form.'

'That accounts for it,' nodded the inspector.

'*Which* accounts for *what?*' demanded Prenderby.

'His lack of control is accounted for by his activities *outside* of Form hours. From careful questioning, it appeared that Chester used to have one or two of the members of junior forms up in his rooms occasionally. It was an open secret among the Third and Second forms — and one which was the subject of many sly winks and mutters. Carfax was one of those — privileged? — boys. After a great deal of questioning he broke down into tears and told us what we wanted to know. That there *was* something between Chester and he, not to mention one or two of the other boys . . .

'Carfax told us that Beasly came to hear about this, and got hold of him and bullied the truth out of him! Carfax was afraid of what would happen, but Beasly told him that if Chester had the sense to see things *his* — Beasly's — way, nothing would happen.'

He looked at Prenderby meditatively.

'So now it's your theory that Beasly was blackmailing Chester, and Chester murdered him to get rid of him?'

'That's it exactly. Fits, doesn't it?'

'Very nicely. But can you *prove* it?'

'We will, once we've got hold of Chester. And that won't be long in happening.'

The inspector got up. 'Just thought I'd drop in and let you know. You seemed so sceptical previously.'

'What is going to happen about Carfax?'

'I've promised the Headmaster we'll hush the affair up as much as possible. Carfax is being sent to his home. But I'm very much afraid that in the case of free news such as this, we've no alternative but to let the papers run it if they wish. We'll do our best — more than that can't be promised.'

'I expect Dr. Wignall feels very badly?'

'He does. He says people won't believe the case of Chester is the *exception* rather than the rule. Says this will reflect badly on all public schools.'

Prenderby nodded, sagely. 'It will, undoubtedly. Why the devil can't people see that the way to curb this sort of thing is coeducation? They have it in America because they're progressive. No harm comes of it there; but if it's as much as suggested in England, people fling up their hands in horror and yell that the boys would be sleeping with the girls!'

'So they would,' said the inspector.

Prenderby shrugged. 'I'm afraid you're as bad as the rest of them, Inspector.'

'I know human nature,' said the inspector. 'I have to, in my job.'

'I think *my* job calls for a certain knowledge of the same thing just as much as yours does. They don't sleep together in the States.'

'That isn't to say the desire isn't there.'

'What of it? It's a normal, healthy desire. A natural one — isn't it?'

But the inspector wasn't to be won over. He left, still shaking his head doubtfully.

Left alone, Prenderby grunted moodily:

'If ever I get a free hand with any school, I'll show 'em!'

★   ★   ★

Mr. Joseph Waltham Lodge, proprietor of the Scarlet Rabbit Public House, was in his early fifties. Mr. Lodge had once been a third-rate touring comic, not entirely unknown in the smaller dumps of the provincial cotton towns. He had a line in wit which had more than once brought him into violent conflict with local watch committees; but Joey Lodge (his stage name), who 'gives you a blue evening' (his bill matter), had known what his audience wanted and given of his plenty.

But alas, the cinema had suddenly grown into audibility, and Mr. Lodge the reverse. A severe attack of laryngitis had scooped him from his beloved boards for almost six months. On his return to the agents' offices he had found theatres closing, going over to moving pictures, all over the country.

Whereupon, with commendable promptitude, he had held court on his capital, and had found that there was sufficient with which to realise his *second* greatest ambition in life. Namely, to own a pub of his own.

So Mr. Lodge had descended upon Munston and established himself firmly in the Scarlet Rabbit.

Until that time it had been a quiet, respectable pub. Joey's loose line in wit had quickly frightened away the better type of customer, leaving the riff-raff of the neighbourhood, who were always assured of being able to speak their minds at the Swill Bin.

Aside from his love of his own person, Joey had another love, almost as strong, for the coin of the realm. He was a collector, and he collected ardently. Any little stunt which would help to swell his already not-inconsiderable funds was welcomed.

And his attentions to the trade to be had from St. Mark's showed a great profit.

It had started with his serving those over eighteen with drinks and a game of billiards. For this the law could not lay its stern hand upon him. They — the seniors — were of legal age to drink, and only their own school had the power to prevent such activities.

But it had not stopped *there*.

Mr. Lodge found he could command a sum of anything from three to four pounds by leasing his back room to the boys, for whatever purpose they might have in mind. Sometimes it was a smoking den, more often an even less laudable attraction.

There was a great element of risk in it for Joey Lodge. But his natural cupidity destroyed his fear of consequences. He had never possessed any striking moral principles, so that aspect of the matter bothered him not one jot.

He did not know Mr. Prenderby by sight. Therefore, when Prenderby walked in one morning, soon after his chat with Mr. Baxter of the Sixth, Lodge was unaware that the Philistines were in the camp.

The bar chanced to be almost deserted since it was some five minutes to three, and almost closing time. Joey Lodge leaned across the counter — he was his own barman — and said, pleasantly enough:

'What can I get yer, Squire?'

Prenderby ordered a light ale and paid for it. After a mouthful he set it down and looked about the bar.

'Not much business?'

'Never is, this time,' said Joey Lodge. 'Gets a bit more crowded later on, see.'

'I shouldn't have thought a pub would pay, in such an out-of-the-way place?' hazarded the stranger to Mr. Lodge.

'Oh, I dunno — I got *sidelines*.' Joey Lodge here paused and rid himself of a deliberate wink.

It was all very deep and meaningful, and Prenderby eyed him closely.

'*Sidelines*, eh?'

'Yes, I get along all right. You strange here?'

'Yes,' admitted Prenderby. 'I'm a stranger *here*.'

Which was not precisely a lie. He was strange to the pub. He had never been into it previously. Joey assumed he was strange to the district, and chuckled.

'Them young rips from the collidge up there,' he said, with a meaningful leer.

'What about them?' Prenderby asked.

Joey grinned again. 'There's a lot of cash in them boyos for a man who knows how to collect it. You'd be surprised at the things they gets up to. I was meself, at first.'

That was all Prenderby had wanted to know. He now shot Mr. Lodge's clay pigeon of revelation down with both barrels.

'What do you charge to rent them the room for a couple of hours?'

'I get about — here! What you talking about?'

Prenderby indicated the passage leading to the back.

'There's a room down there. I know all about it. You rent it to seniors for exorbitant sums. Right?'

'Don't you go sayin' things like that 'ere,' said Mr. Lodge aggrievedly. 'I never 'eard the likes of that!'

There was contempt in Prenderby's voice when next he spoke.

'Don't get excited, Mr. Lodge.'

187

Joey Lodge leaned across the counter and stared at his accuser.

'Who *are* you, any'ow?'

'My name's Prenderby, I'm the master of North House at St. Mark's . . . '

'Blimey!' gasped Joey, his eyes opening wider. ''Ere — you told me you was a *stranger*!'

Prenderby nodded. 'I told you that I was strange here. I *am* strange here.'

Joey Lodge recovered himself after a moment. 'I don't admit nothin', see. I don't know nothin' about what you're talkin' about. An' you can't prove nothin'.'

'I imagine I could prove a lot if I wished to,' said the master of North House, slowly. 'As it happens, that wasn't my purpose in calling upon you. I know what goes on here, Lodge. I got it from one of my most truthful seniors. And I have this to say: because of certain considerations which *you* need not know, I have decided to say nothing about this affair — *this time*. In return, I shall require your word — not that that counts for much — that you will not encourage, or even permit, the seniors to drink here. You will personally bar all schoolboys from the premises. You will definitely never rent that back room to any one of them again.'

'You're givin' an 'ell of a lot of orders, Mister. If those who're over eighteen want to have a pail o' suds 'ere at my place, why should *I* stop 'em? I ain't breakin' any laws.'

'You'll stop them because if I see any boy from St. Mark's at your premises again, I will not hold my hand any longer. In short order, Lodge, you will find yourself inside a local police station charged with keeping a disorderly house — for minors!'

Joey Lodge was deflated. He seemed to sag visibly.

Then: 'I never done anythin' what you say, guv'nor. But — if it'll make yer any happier — if it's what you want — I'll give you my word.'

'I wouldn't expect you to honour your word,' said Prenderby. 'At the same time, I warn you again that if there is any repetition of the behaviour — '

'There won't be.'

Mr. Prenderby nodded. 'I hope not — for *your* sake. Goodbye, Mr. Lodge.'

He went out, leaving Joey Lodge reclining weakly upon the counter. After a while he muttered: 'Strewth! I'll 'ave to watch my step — don't want any bluebottles buzzing round 'ere — more especially not *now*!'

And for some reason, although he was supposed to be alone in the pub, he directed an apprehensive look along the passage and up the stairs to a room door which could be seen on the landing.

* * *

Frank Chester paced nervously up and down his room, with a ceaseless, monotonous stride.

His mind was still reeling from the enormity of the thing he had done in running away. Why hadn't he just brazened it out? It was sure to look worse for him in the long run. And sooner or later they were bound to catch him.

He was not a strong man, physically or

mentally. He was a man inclined to a great indulgence in self-pity. At the moment he felt no one cared *what* became of him, that every man's hand was against him — except, of course, the hand of Joey Lodge.

He and Joey had similar depraved tastes. They both thought the same brand of obscene joke was funny, and both had minds which could crawl under a caterpillar, bent double.

Strange contrast — one a Varsity man, the other dragged up by the scruff of his neck in the slum lands of Liverpool.

But their mutual friendship had grown since the day when Lodge had taken over the pub. Chester had been a customer then, and several other of the masters. Then, he had been young and careless. The other masters had gradually found Lodge distasteful and had drifted away to more congenial haunts for their evening tankard. But Chester had stayed on.

Perhaps, he thought, the reason for that strong attraction was because they were both 'queer'. They didn't mention the fact to each other; but, Chester reflected, dog can tell dog. It hadn't taken him ten minutes of conversation with Joey Lodge to know what sort of reputation he had built up for himself backstage. By several of the other touring acts, he had been known as 'Queenie Lodge'. The name implied no disgrace — Joey's contemporaries of the theatre were broad-minded. And they commented on how well he played the Dame in pantomime.

Chester guessed, although the subject had not been spoken in all their years of friendship, that Joey had also sized him up as being of the same breed.

Thinking along those lines brought him back to his present trouble.

Suppose the police were to dig out the facts about him? If Lemster, or Carfax, or any of the others, talked —

He shivered, cursed himself again for taking chances like that. Cursed himself for letting that little rat Beasly get the better of him.

In one way, he was glad Beasly had been murdered. But he knew that he was in grave danger of hanging for it. There was too much evidence against him.

What use would it be to tell them he *hadn't* killed Beasly, that he'd paid Beasly blackmail money for many months, but had never even dreamed of taking such a way out?

He stopped thinking, and jumped nervously as the door opened. Joey Lodge stood there, regarding him.

'Frank, you got to get movin' as quick as possible,' said Joey, without mincing matters. 'There's been a bloke from the school in the pub . . . '

Chester's face paled.

'Bloke called Prenderby — '

'*Prenderby?* He — he doesn't suspect I'm here, does he?'

'No — he don't suspect nothin' like that. Only he knows I've been earnin' a bit on the side by rentin' that back room and such. He reckons he won't split, but it's too risky for me to 'ave any secrets on the premises. You got to leave, Frank.'

Chester sank back onto the bed.

'But where — where can I go? How? And *when?* I haven't more than a few pounds — '

'I thought of that. 'Ere — 'ere's twenty

quid. You can pay it me back sometime — any time you're able.'

It was a strange gesture from Joey Lodge. It proved that though he had no morality, decency, or respectability, he did have *one* thing that the possessors of the above often lacked. *Loyalty*.

They sat down on the edge of the bed to talk it over, and when Joey left to open up for the evening, it was arranged that Chester should make an effort to get to London and lose himself in the cosmopolitan crowds there . . .

12

Frank Chester Makes his Exit

Brooks came into the Masters' Common Room in North House the following afternoon with an excited face. He buttonholed Prenderby.

'Heard the news about Chester? I just had it from the messenger boy from the village.'

Prenderby began to display interest. 'I haven't heard anything about Chester. What is it?'

'They believe he was seen at Branshoot last night, taking the late train for London.'

Prenderby whistled thoughtfully. 'Meaning he's only just left the district?'

'That's how it looks. Someone reported it to the police — saw his photograph in the paper.'

'Then they've got his trail?'

They had his trail only too well. As long

as Frank Chester had remained at the Scarlet Rabbit, out of sight and sound, he would have been safe enough. But once he left his lair, like a pack of hounds closing in on a panting fox, the forces of law began to narrow down the circle in the centre of which they had him cornered.

At that precise moment, from reports, the London C.I.D. knew the wanted man was somewhere in the central London area. It was only a question of time now before he fell into their hands.

Haggard, haunted, tired and dishevelled, Frank Chester, looking little like the dapper master of St. Mark's that he had been only a short time before, moved wearily about the shabbier portions of Soho. Every blue uniform he saw brought a gulp, every glance directed towards him sent a chill of fear along his craven spine.

Then, with the arrival of the evening papers, he found that the banner headlines glared out in a million hands:

SCHOOLMASTER SUSPECT
AT LARGE IN LONDON!

And beneath the headlines, a large and clear photograph of himself!

He had been wrong to come to London, he knew that now. Far from being a help to him, the crowds were a danger, a continuing menace. He had to get away from the crowded central part of the city. Anywhere, somewhere where it was quieter.

Elstree, Uxbridge, Richmond —

He realised he was in one of the small back streets running off Piccadilly. From a restaurant on his right came the appetising odour of cooking food; a few passers-by were browsing over a second-hand book stall outside a tiny shop. A heavily-painted girl was laughing and joking with a soldier as they walked towards the end of the street.

The shops were beginning to close. It was almost five-thirty. In a few minutes London would make ready to give itself up to the pleasures of the evening. The busy, bustling atmosphere of the daytime would give way to the glamour of the show-going populace; the raucous cries of novelty sellers on the corners; the neon-lighted cafés and milk bars; the stands of casual sellers of cheap, lurid literature; and the cracked, wheezing voices of the flower sellers trying to palm off winter carnations at two shillings a bloom.

Already he could see the line of a queue beginning to form at the top of the street.

He wanted to wait until it was dark — but he dared not. When darkness fell, London's policemen kept even sharper watch.

He decided his best chance was to make a move now. Get away with the final hordes of home-goers, before the suburbanites began to drift back to town for the evening's round.

He drew his hat low down over his face, adjusted his scarf so that it concealed his chin, and with head held forward, went out up the street and into Piccadilly.

He looked longingly towards a Lyons' Corner House, then turned with a sigh and walked towards the Underground entrance. He tried not to think how infernally hungry he was. It seemed as if he had never eaten and would never eat again. His legs felt positively weak.

Every pedestrian who looked in his direction he saw as a threat to his freedom. Every careless eye which alighted on his hurrying figure he imagined to be charged with suspicion and menace. At any second, he expected to feel the weighty hand of one of London's guardians of the peace falling heavily upon his shoulder.

He hurried his steps and gained the entrance to Piccadilly Tube Station. He went down hastily, allowing himself to follow the crowd.

He paused hesitantly at the barrier, fumbled in his pocket until he had produced the correct change for a sixpenny ticket. He went to the machine and plugged this in; then with his face still half-concealed, passed by the ticket collector.

He stood on the escalator, holding to the moving rail for support. His face was damp with perspiration, the dew of sheer terror.

He caught a snatch of conversation between a Cockney and his wife who were arguing in front of him.

'Why didn't yer stay wiv the bluddy barrer, then?'

'Yus, it's *likely*, ain't it? While you go sittin' on your bluddy arse, swillin' yer pig's ear! Yus, cop me *doin'* it. And I only moved a minute to 'ave a word with Maggie . . . '

'Leave Maggie to look arter 'er own ruddy stall, an' you arter yours.'

The woman spat, viciously. 'One o' these days I'll swing for you, 'Arry, sure as me name's Lil 'Arris!'

Swing — *swing* — the word whirled round Chester's brain until he wanted to scream.

He stumbled from the escalator, catching his foot against the guard.

He walked blindly to the second staircase, allowed it to carry him down. Now the dulled rumble and rattle of the train was pounding in his ears. Hardly knowing where he was going, he lurched unsteadily along with the crowd.

He became entangled with those going

to the Uxbridge-Hounslow line . . .

He found himself carried onto the platform, and stood in the mass awaiting a train.

As the approaching rattle and hiss filled the tube, a hand reached his shoulder. He started. Turned.

No mistaking the stern-faced man there. *Detective* stood out on him a mile.

'I'd like a word with you — *Chester*.'

It had *happened*! And Frank Chester, half-insane, able to think of nothing other than getting away from that raincoated C.I.D. man, suddenly dodged frantically through a gap in the crowd.

The next moment he was running crazily along the narrow space between travellers and track —

The train screamed harshly on, into the station . . .

★   ★   ★

The inspector from Barnshoot called in to see Prenderby the same evening. Brooks was with Prenderby at the time, correcting some Latin exercises. The inspector entered in answer to their call, and helped himself liberally from the bottle on the table to which Prenderby motioned him.

'Didn't know you schoolmaster chaps were allowed to have liquor on the premises,' he observed.

'It isn't customary,' Prenderby agreed. 'Or should I say, it isn't customary — *officially?* What brought *you* over, Inspector?'

The officer sipped his drink, and adopted a superior manner again. It was his nature to laud it a little.

'Just came to tell you I was *right* when I said we'd get to Chester shortly. We did. They took him in London tonight.'

'Does he still protest his innocence, then?' Prenderby asked.

'He can't. He's *dead.*'

'Dead?' It was a gasp from both Brooks and Prenderby.

The Inspector smiled. 'What do you want me to say? 'As a doornail'?'

'But how . . . ?' Prenderby said.

'One of our plain-clothes men apprehended him in Piccadilly Circus subway station. He tried to make a bolt for it as a train was coming in — he went off the edge of the platform and under the wheels. He was pretty badly mangled, but there was proof of identity on him.'

'So that closes the case?' Brooks wanted to know.

'It's closed as far as we're concerned.'

'And you're perfectly *satisfied*?' Prenderby asked.

The inspector frowned. 'Why shouldn't I be satisfied? The motive, opportunity, evidence . . . all implicated Chester. Then his bolt — '

Prenderby said: 'You needn't reiterate all that for me. I simply asked a question — are you perfectly satisfied that Frank Chester murdered Beasly of this school?'

The inspector was reluctant to say it. But eventually he committed himself in a low tone:

'Yes.'

'You'll drop the investigation?'

'Unless some fresh light is thrown on the murder.'

'But what about the girl — Gregg's daughter?' Brooks wanted to know.

'We're still pursuing that case. It isn't closed yet. Can't be sure Chester did the two of them. Knowing what we now do about Chester, it isn't likely *he'd* be interested in women. Mark you, we can't be sure of anything. And that killing was a long time ago.'

'I understood you C.I.D. men *never* gave up?'

'Nor do we. I've known cases of a murderer having been caught and convicted after a period of ten to fifteen years.'

He looked at Prenderby whimsically.

'I expect you're still dissatisfied?'

'I am. With the whole thing. And I think Chester was damned unlucky. He didn't deserve to die.'

'He brought that upon himself.'

The inspector got to his feet. 'Well, I thought I'd let you know and obtain your reactions. As far as I'm concerned there's nothing more to be said. But — ' He stopped, and looked at Prenderby and Brooks for five or six seconds. Then he went on, confidentially: 'But *unofficially*, if you do happen on anything connected with this case that looks as if it might be of interest — I'd be glad to know. Good night.'

★ ★ ★

Miss Scotch, Headmistress of Munston Girls' School, stopped abruptly.

Miss Scotch had been Headmistress of the school since its inception in 1928. They had been twenty quiet, uneventful years. Twenty years of serenity and bliss, unmarred by any major disturbances. On the whole, reflected Miss Scotch, the girls she had presided over had been a good-natured and well-behaved bunch. To a certain extent she felt she could trust them.

She was aware that, with the heartlessness common to young people, they called her 'Old Gammy' amongst themselves. But she did not resent this very much. They had to have some nickname for authority. It was natural. And she *was* gammy, anyhow. Her left leg had somehow failed to attain the same length as her right. It caused her to walk with a stiff limp.

Miss Scotch was not an unkind woman. She could, on occasion, be very strict and merciless, as a number of past pupils of Munston had found out to their sorrow. But in the main she felt a deep responsibility towards her youthful charges, and towards her staff, too.

She was a matronly woman of about fifty-eight. She wore pince-nez with an air, and terrible were the glances she could deliver from them when the need arose.

Her bloodless lips were perhaps a trifle too thin for the rest of her round face. Her teeth were false but looked natural.

Her nose was puttylike, red at the tip, which made the girls pass skittish remarks about old Gammy being a sly 'boozer'. They were not far wrong. She was. She told herself it was medicine; actually, she had never felt ill in her life. Whatever happened, she had to have her double Scotch before retiring at night. The other teachers at Munston guessed the truth. They, not as unkind as the girls where physical disability was concerned, called her amongst themselves 'Whisky'.

This was derived both from her habit and name.

There had been times when the life had tried her sorely. When worry had caused yet another hair of her once jet-black locks to turn grey within the space of a few days. Or, at least, so she was fond of asserting. She often said to the gym mistress:

'Dear me, Miss Nightingale, these girls will have me really *snow-white* before I'm sixty!'

She refused to admit, even to herself, that the grey hairs were the natural ravages of time. It had nothing to do with pigmentation. It was the worry of being mistress of Munston.

Perhaps her most arduous task had been seeing her school stay above reproach, morally. Unlike Mr. Prenderby, Miss Scotch thought that sort of thing was — revolting! No man had ever even kissed *her* — and had one tried, he would have fainted with horror.

She had never known the urge of the flesh. She could not begin to appreciate what others saw in it. That Miss Storm, for instance — the Third Form mistress — had got herself into trouble with a local man and married him. Now she could be seen about the town, reduced to absolute poverty and discomfort. And still she seemed happy.

Miss Scotch really couldn't understand it. No man was really worth a fig, she was wont to say, to her staff.

She had a number of worn clichés, which she trotted out for airing whenever the subject of men came up. Be it gossip, scandal, or surmise, Miss Scotch was always ready with a quotation:

'*All* men are alike,' she would say, 'the woman *always* pays'; and again, 'I don't know what you *see* in them.'

She often thought of Craven, the porter she had had to dismiss many years ago. Craven, who had been discovered peering in at the Sixth Form window whilst the girls were undressing!

She had, since then, not having come into contact with many other men since her arrival at Munston, been inclined to judge *all* men by Craven. Peering, depraved beings, with unclean, lustful minds.

She moderated her views in two instances only. Her long-dead father — she was fond of claiming him to be 'a *saint*' — and her younger brother, a London businessman. These, she was convinced, were the only two decent men born in the past hundred years.

Holding such views — she would have been highly indignant if anyone had dared to suggest that her views were highly distorted — as these, on life and men and the things they did to women, she was naturally very careful where the girls were concerned.

It was only after much persuasion upon the part of Dr. Wignall of St. Mark's that she had eventually agreed to permit her senior girls to attend the Friday dances at the roadhouse. She had a great respect for Dr. Wignall's mental abilities. She considered him an extremely capable and clever Headmaster. At the same time, she made no reservations in his case — she told herself that, in *other* ways, he was probably just as depraved as the rest of his sex. Or had been when younger.

Although it had been against her better judgment, Dr. Wignall had talked her into allowing her girls to attend a dance. He had stressed that there should be some social life between the two schools. She had agreed at length to give this idea a trial. So far, it seemed to have worked excellently. The Munston girls had a fresh interest in life. They began to take pride in being always neat and clean and tidy. She disapproved of the fact that they had begun to use more make-up, but found she could hardly curb this feminine vanity unless it became excessive.

But with the advent of Marjorie Payne to the school, a cloud had come upon her horizon.

Marjorie was the daughter of influential London socialites. She was a pupil of whom Miss Scotch was justly proud. Unlike St. Mark's, Munston Girls'. was *not* a well-known school. It was a modest little affair, designed to catch the overflow from the more impressive Colleges for the Daughters of Gentlefolk.

Marjorie, she had thought, had been a good overflow. Her parents, the Paynes, were reputed to be friends of Royalty. They were always being photographed for Society papers — 'Mr. John Augustus Payne and friend at the Masonic reception' or 'Mrs. Payne and party at Lady V — 's charity fete'.

Miss Scotch had met Mr. and Mrs. Payne and found them charming. Their daughter Marjorie she had found less so. It quickly became apparent that Marjorie was, as the other girls put it, 'a case'.

Marjorie had flirted outrageously with the messenger boys from the village, even when she had been only fifteen years old. Marjorie had been seen and reported as swimming in the nude in the nearby river. Marjorie had got her name into the London papers when she had been entangled in a restaurant scene during her holiday in London. Marjorie had been stubborn about wearing the school uniform at first, although later she had succumbed. Marjorie had led all of the mistresses a song and dance.

Miss Scotch was anxiously awaiting an opportunity to tell her nicely that she must leave school, but no excuse presented itself.

Marjorie, Miss Scotch learned when she had been there three terms, had already been expelled from three schools. She was a high-spirited girl, given to demanding her own way a great deal; and if she didn't have permission to do what she wanted, she did it anyhow. Although, so stern had been the lecture she had received from her father on her last expulsion, she had decided to go more carefully at Munston. She felt that otherwise she might wind up in a convent in France.

It was Marjorie who had now caused Miss Scotch to stop and start in such an unseemly fashion. Marjorie, wearing fashionable clothing, extremely high heels, plenty of make-up, and a precocious little hat perched on the side of her curly head.

There was a very strict rule at Munston Girls' that during term-time *school uniform only* should be worn. And now Miss Scotch bore down upon the rule-breaker with a grim visage and lowered brows.

'Marjorie! *Where* are you going?'

Marjorie had been sneaking quietly behind the school to gain the main road via the playing fields. Now she flushed and straightened up. She fumbled for an excuse and found one almost immediately.

'I'm sorry, Miss Scotch — I was going to the town of Branshoot.'

'To *Branshoot*?' queried Miss Scotch, her eyebrows doing a jig. 'In *that* costume?'

Her eyes fixed awesomely upon the split skirt, and the length of leg above the knee which peeped demurely therefrom.

'You are *aware* of the rule which prohibits the wearing of any other apparel than that authorised by the school, Marjorie?'

'Yes, Miss Scotch . . . but . . . ' She paused, and had a happy inspiration to appeal to the snob in her Head: 'But I have an awfully *important* engagement, Miss Scotch . . . a friend of mine, *Lady* Pamela Wetherby, the daughter of the Duchess of Gore, is passing through Branshoot today. She wants me to take tea with her at Harper's stores. I could hardly turn up in school uniform, *could* I, Miss Scotch?' she finished appealingly.

Miss Scotch was somewhat mollified. It was nice to have her girls consorting with titled people. She had never heard of the Duchess in question, nor her honourable daughter, but there were lots of Duchesses she knew nothing about in England.

More graciously, she nodded. 'I understand, my dear child. But why did you not *tell me* of your engagement, and ask my permission? Better still, why did you not invite your friend *here* to tea?'

Marjorie lied convincingly. 'But she's in rather a hurry, Miss Scotch. She'll have only a half-hour to spare — and I didn't get her telegram until a half-hour ago.'

Miss Scotch relented. Hesitated, and then: 'In that case, my dear, you may go. But be sure to be back for locking-up.'

Marjorie nodded, grateful to escape without being asked to show the nonexistent telegram.

'I will, Miss Scotch — and thank you ever so much.'

Miss Scotch, almost genial, waved her

on her way. Marjorie walked towards the front gates, secure in the knowledge she had permission now. Questing schoolgirl eyes followed her, some of them envious. At the gates Phyllis was standing with a bunch of the form. They regarded Marjorie with surprise.

'Ouch, girls! Look at *that*!'

'Solomon in all his glory was not arrayed in such as these,' misquoted someone else.

'You'll catch it if old Gammy spots you,'

'I won't,' said Marjorie serenely. 'I happen to have old Gammy's *permish* to wear these. Phyll, I'm going to Branshoot to — to meet some friends. I'll be back about six — or just afterwards. Like to walk along to the bus stop and meet me?'

Phyllis nodded. 'Of course, Marge.'

Marjorie said, 'Thanks,' and walked on. She caught the bus to Branshoot, arriving there just as the town hall clock struck five-fifteen, but her steps didn't lead in the direction of Harper's stores, or anywhere near there. Instead, she cut off the main road; and by dint of much walking, finally found a quiet, sedate, tree-lined street on the outskirts, with a house which bore a brass plate tacked to its door: 'Doctor Henry Billings'.

She pushed the gate open and walked the few steps to the door. She thumbed the bell.

A maid answered the door, and Marjorie murmured: 'Could I see the Doctor, please?'

'Surgery's at six,' said the maid, churlishly. 'Unless you've an appointment?'

'I have — '

The maid opened the door and stood aside. 'Come in then . . . '

13

Marjorie Learns the Worst!

She was shown into a small waiting room liberally supplied with the usual outdated periodicals. She picked one up listlessly, then put it down again unlooked-at. She studied, very intensely, the gas fire and the cane-backed chairs, the large flat leather divan which looked as if it might have been used to lay out the dead. She shivered, unaccountably.

The maid had taken her name in to the doctor. She hoped he would see her —

The maid came back and opened the door, and stood aside without speaking. Marjorie followed her along a short passage, through a bead curtain, and into a rather dingy room at the back of the house, overlooking the garden.

There was a flat-topped desk against the wall, littered with Health Insurance prescription pads and panel notes. There was a high leather and chromium examination table. An adjustable light above it. A smaller table littered with stethoscope, spatula, and a few instruments she was unable to name. A door led into a dispensary. It was half-open and the rows of bottles could be seen.

The doctor was sitting at his desk writing on a prescription pad. As she entered he said, without looking up:

'Sit down, young lady.'

He might have been about thirty-eight years of age, but he looked older. His voice and movements were those of a man in his thirties, but his face was brown — unhealthily brown — and greying hair had receded so far back from the front of his head that it was hardly visible when you looked straight at him. He was inclined to stoop a little, and his body, under the sober grey cloth of his suit, was thin.

Marjorie sat down. He continued to write for a few minutes in silence, then he blotted the pad and thrust it to the back of the desk.

'The maid told me you said you had an *appointment?*'

Marjorie flushed. 'I — I've come a good way to see you Doctor, and I couldn't possibly be here at six ... I couldn't attend the morning surgery, either.'

He raised his eyebrows, but didn't ask her why. She couldn't have given any reasonable explanation. Couldn't have told him that the school had its own doctor, but that she could hardly take her present trouble to him. Couldn't even tell him she was a schoolgirl — hence her reason for not wearing the school uniform.

'I dislike people saying they have an appointment when they *haven't*,' he told her.

'But, please, Doctor — it's important. I'm sorry I had to lie ... '

He nodded. 'Very well, since you're here. What is the trouble, Miss Payne?'

She told him; he pursed his lips, and indicated the table. 'I'll have to make an examination. Just prepare yourself, please ... '

There was no modesty about Marjorie. She prepared herself rapidly. Her heart was thumping — not with self-consciousness, but with fear of what he would find.

He didn't waste very much time on her. After a few moments he frowned, said: 'You can get dressed now.'

As she finished fastening her blouse with fumbling fingers, he spoke. He was leaning over the desk writing again, and he said without looking up,

'Are you married?'

He seemed to have guessed she wasn't, and she didn't see any point in lying about it. 'No, Doctor.'

'You have had intercourse recently?'

She hesitated, then, 'Ye-es.'

'I see. Well, young lady, I'm afraid you're going to have a baby!'

Now that it had happened, she took it very calmly. She'd really suspected, for the last three months, that that was the trouble. The worst of the shock had been eased.

'You're sure, Doctor?'

'Quite sure.'

'Doctor — ' she said, moving over towards the desk, 'I — I don't want it. It will mean terrible disgrace for me — '

He sighed. 'Miss Payne, if I had a pound for each time I heard those words, I'd be a rich man.'

She pleaded, 'But please — couldn't you *do* something? Give me something? To — to — I'd pay well.'

He swung round in the swivel chair suddenly and looked at her angrily. He was *very* angry.

'I'm an ordinary medical practitioner, young woman, and I haven't any intention of becoming an abortionist. If you don't want the stigma of having a fatherless child, you should have refrained from indulging your emotions. If you call the tune, the piper may reasonably expect to be reckoned with.'

Marjorie wilted. Quite unexpectedly, she found herself crying. He noticed it, and his voice softened.

'Come now, it isn't as bad as all that . . . '

She mumbled: 'Could you — could you tell me of anyone who might — be able to help me?'

He frowned again. 'I would advise you

to put thoughts of that nature completely from your mind. Since you are in the unhappy position of being pregnant, resign yourself to facing the ordeal bravely. Does the young man know of your condition?'

'I — yes.'

'He will stand by you? He loves you?'

'Oh, yes, he'll marry me. But — '

The doctor stood up, smiled, and placed a hand on her shoulder, comfortingly.

'It isn't such a great disgrace, these days,' he told her. 'Your parents may well be upset, but they will not hold it against you once the first shock is over. Cheer up . . . your case is not *so* unusual. I have a similar case almost every week. Foolish girls like yourself who have let their love for a man blind them to moral responsibility. Perhaps you would prefer it if *I* explained to your parents . . . ?'

She said, hastily: 'It's kind of you, Doctor, but I would prefer to explain myself . . . '

'As you wish. Now, you must attend a pre-natal clinic regularly in future. They will help you over what is always a very difficult period, and will advise you on the best way to prepare for the baby. You are not afraid of the confinement itself, are you?' he asked, noticing how her hands trembled as she put on her coat.

'Oh, no. That doesn't worry me. It's just — well, just the explanations.'

'I would advise you to see your young man first, and make arrangements for your marriage. Then get him to see your parents with you.'

As she walked back to the bus stop, she was trying hard to think calmly. No sense in getting into a fluster about it. Eric would have to stand by her. It would mean they'd both have to leave school, but that would be a blessing. She wondered if she loved Eric, and would go on loving him? Then she shrugged. Her feelings for him weren't very deep, she realised. Physical attraction and nothing more. But perhaps they *could* make a go of it; and if not, there was always divorce at some suitably distant date.

For the coming baby she had no feelings at all. She felt vaguely annoyed that she had been caught, and a little angry with Eric. She had been sure it couldn't happen to her. Now it had, she was smarting under a feeling of injustice. Hundreds of girls got away with it — why had she been singled out for the shame and misery?

She laughed suddenly. Shame and misery! That was good. It was taking a conventional, almost Victorian view of the matter. It seemed worse because they were both at school, but really she *was* a woman. Being at school didn't make you any less likely to slip than being a worker. She had a heart, and a mind, and various other items. She had the usual physical equipment. She wasn't any different to the girl in the shop, or the girl in the factory or office, underneath. Nor was Eric of a different pattern to the mill-hand or the farmer's boy, or the youth in a shipping office. She wasn't sure how *his* parents would take it. But she knew that, after the first disbelief, her own mother and father would stand by her through anything. If Eric's folks created trouble, her father would give

Eric a job with his firm, and everything would be all right.

By the time the bus rolled along, she had recovered her former poise and cynical outlook. She wasn't going to allow herself to break up in such a fashion. Behaving like a character from some nineteenth-century melodrama wasn't going to make things any better!

★ ★ ★

Phyllis was waiting for her at the bus stop as promised. As they began the short walk back to the school, she said:

'Have a nice time with your friends, Marge?'

Marjorie laughed. 'I'd forgotten I told the girls that tale. Keep it dark, Phyll; but the fact is, I didn't go to see any friends in Branshoot. That was just for the benefit of Miss Scotch and the girls.'

Phyllis' eyes widened. 'Then where did you go? Not to — Eric Baxter? Did you?'

'Not that either. I went to the doctor's . . . '

'Which doctor's?' queried Phyllis, bewilderedly.

'Oh, I couldn't say. I just walked until I found a little M.D. on the outskirts of the town. I wanted one who wasn't too central, who was out of the way.'

'But why didn't you go to the school doctor?'

'I couldn't. Not with *my* complaint, darling.'

Phyllis shook her head. 'I don't know what you're talking about, Marjorie. You aren't ill, are you?'

'I never felt fitter,' said Marjorie, with a smile. 'Apart, of course, from a little *morning sickness*. That's quite natural and nothing to worry about.'

Phyllis jumped. 'Morn — *morning sickness?* Please, Marge, don't joke — '

Marjorie stopped walking and touched her arm. She looked at her steadily. 'I'm *not* joking, Phyllis.'

'But you didn't tell me — '

'I wanted to find out first — for certain.'

'And you have found out? But Marge, you *can't* mean — '

'Yes I do, Phyll. I'm going to have a baby. I'm more than three months pregnant.'

'Oh, no — Marge, it's too *awful* — you *can't* — '

'I'm afraid we have no say in the matter. I can, and I will, have to go through with it, Phyll.'

Phyllis said, in a small voice, 'Eric's?'

'The same.'

'Does he know?'

'He doesn't even suspect. It will be your own unpleasant duty, Phyllis, to bring the matter to his attention tomorrow night at the dance.'

'I couldn't, I just *couldn't.*'

'You will, darling. For my sake. And you won't have to *say* anything, anyway. I'll write a letter to him. You'll just hand it to him, and wait for his answer. You see, we have an arrangement that we won't be seen together for some time. This alters everything, of course. I'll have to see him, and thrash the matter out.'

She grinned and pinched Phyllis' arm. 'Cheer up — the skies won't fall, Phyll. Women have had babies before. And I'll brazen it out all right. I did ask the Doctor if he could get rid of it for me . . . '

'You *didn't*!'

'He said he couldn't. Got quite annoyed about it, too. I'm afraid I'm stuck with it now.'

'But you said — you said there wasn't any risk of that with you and Eric. You said — '

' — he was always too careful? I know I did, Phyll. I must have been mistaken, mustn't I? I'm quite annoyed with Eric about that. I'll have a few well-chosen words to say to him when I see him.'

'What will you do?'

'We'll have to get married, I'm very much afraid.'

'Will Eric want that?'

Marjorie plucked at her bag-snap thoughtfully for a second.

'Yes, I think he will. Poor Eric, he'll curse himself for this. He's very fond of me, Phyll. Much fonder than I am of him.'

'There'll be an awful scandal, Marge.'

Marjorie shook her head. 'There

228

needn't be any scandal. No need for anyone other than Eric and his folks, and you and a few people, to know anything about it. Eric can just leave school quietly, and I'll do the same. We'll be married secretly in a registry office, and there you are. It's quite simple.'

Phyllis touched her hand. 'Marge, aren't you frightened of having the baby?'

Marjorie laughed lightly. 'Why should I be frightened of that? It's a natural function.'

They drew near to the school gates. One of the girls called: 'You look as if you've had a high old time with your friends, Marge.'

'Quite enjoyable,' said Marjorie, as she passed on.

★ ★ ★

Pritchet of the Fourth was bent industriously above an open book on the study table. To anyone peering in, he would have seemed to have been deep in an arduous translation for the evening's prep.

The actual fact, though, was very far from that.

The opened book was a regulation copy of the Bible. Pritchet, with his usual habit, was going through it compiling a list of the obscene and immoral passages.

Basset, his study mate, came in, and flopped into a chair. He eyed Pritchet with considerable amazement.

'Not mugging?' he queried, unbelievingly.

Pritchet chuckled. 'In a way, you might say I was. I say, Basset, it says here that . . . '

He related the unsavoury paragraph he had just found, and Basset's honest, open face wrinkled in contempt.

'Why don't you *grow up*, Pritch?' he enquired disgustedly. 'You've got a one-track mind. Always looking for filth of some kind, aren't you?'

Pritchet was highly indignant at this unheralded attack. 'Why, you cheeky ass, *you've* listened to jokes and laughed at them as much as I have.'

'I admit that. But damn it, Pritch, there's a *limit*.'

Pritchet looked at the opened Bible, and understanding dawned.

'I see what you mean now. I forgot you were a religious chump, Basset.'

Pritchet was very fond of declaiming his atheism to anyone who could be persuaded to listen. Next to the recital of coarse jokes, it was his greatest pleasure.

Basset changed the subject. He had no desire for one of the long, wrangling arguments which Pritchet was so fond of having.

'Hear about old Gregg?'

Pritchet displayed interest. 'No. What about Gregg?'

Basset grinned. 'Seems he isn't satisfied that Chester killed his daughter. He's still roaming the woods at night, they say. One of the prefects spotted him going out the other night — looking as if he was in for an all-night session, they say. Thick boots, and a heavy coat.'

'The silly old chump. I think he's off his rocker, Bassy. He won't find anything in the woods.'

Basset nodded sagely. 'It's my opinion they'll have to sit on his napper and howl for the yellow van eventually,' he said. 'You can see it in his eyes — and the way he walks round. I don't think he's ever smiled since he came back here this term.'

Pritchet closed the Bible. 'He hasn't, I'm sure of it. I expect it's something to do with neuroses and that sort of bilge. Left him with some mental kink, eh? Those psychiatrist chappies could put him right, I dare say. Why doesn't he see one?'

Basset nodded. 'Mind, it would have been a hell of a shock for anyone losing a daughter in *that* way. They say she was in a bad state altogether — '

Pritchet muttered, 'They never gave details of her injuries. What do you suppose was done to her?'

He looked avidly and speculatively at Basset, who frowned and looked the other way.

'There you go again, Pritch. Whatever it was, it was pretty awful, I expect. She must have gone through hell.'

Basset dragged the conversation back forcibly to Gregg.

'Tell you what, unless old Gregg stops this prowling of his, the Head'll get to hear, and put an end to it. Can't have a master of St. Mark's wandering in the woods all night. For *nothing*.'

Pritchet chuckled softly. 'Maybe it *isn't* for nothing? What if he was in the habit of meeting one of the tarts from the village down there, and was working this mental stunt as a cover?'

Basset grinned hugely at this idea, and grunted: 'Pritchet, your mind's been dangled in the sewers . . . '

And Pritchet chuckled: 'I wouldn't deny it, old top.'

14

Prenderby Falls in Love

The dance at the roadhouse was well-attended as usual. The dance room was separated from the rest of the place, including the licensed bar, and only soft drinks were permitted on such nights as the girls and boys of the respective schools attended.

Tonight there was a good turnout.

Even Miss Scotch had come along, and was now seated at the far end of the room, discussing with Miss Nightingale the prospect of May Viner carrying off the Junior Latin Prize.

The boys of St. Mark's mingled freely with the girls of Munton. But there was one notable absence — namely, Marjorie Payne.

That in itself was surprising. Usually she was the centre of all eyes, and always closely attended by Baxter. But Marjorie had decided it would be better not to go at all, after the matter of Gregg in the woods; if he happened to be at the dance, it was likely he would recognise her again.

Phyllis was there. She carried a note from Marjorie, tucked away down the top of her brassiere. She dreaded the ordeal before her, but she was staunch in her determination to carry it through for the sake of her unlucky friend.

In a way, she felt sorry for Baxter; it was evident to her that he was very much in love with Marjorie — and although she was Marge's friend, and loyal, she had to admit to herself that Marge wasn't worth an honest love.

Nor did she blame Baxter for the situation in which Marge found herself now. She knew well enough that her friend was a temptress of the first order; and it would have needed a very strong-willed man to have held out against her many charms.

Baxter was present. She spotted him when she came into the room. He was standing at one side, clearly ill at ease. His eyes continually wandered to the door in search of Marjorie. Although he thought it wisest for them not to meet, he still hoped she would come, if only for him to see her again and exchange a smile and a nod.

His eyes fastened upon Phyllis. He smiled.

She sat down on a bench and smiled back, faintly.

The band struck up a quickstep, and Baxter at once hurried from his position and came towards her.

'Do you mind dancing this, Phyllis?'

'I'd like to, Eric.'

They got up, and joined the swirling throng on the floor. As they danced round Baxter said:

'Phyll . . . how is Marjorie? I see she isn't here.'

'She thought it would be better . . .'

'Oh. Yes — perhaps it is — old Gregg — '

He broke off, not certain how much Phyllis knew about his affair with her friend.

After a while, Phyllis said:

'She asked me to give you a note. Eric,

this is very serious. She wants an answer. I'll take it when I go back.'

She blushed, and wished she hadn't consigned that note to the care of her brassiere now. But the lights dimmed as the spotlight came into play, and she fumbled it out and pressed it into Eric's hands.

He said, 'Thanks. It was sporting of you to bother.'

'Please hurry and read it, and give me your answer. It's so dreadfully important.'

Baxter said: 'Yes — I will.'

The dance ended, and he retired to a corner to read the note. His fingers were eager as he opened it, his face expectant.

Then, as he read, his face went white. His fingers tightened convulsively on the paper, and he gasped: 'Oh, Lord!'

The note was blunt, like its writer. Marjorie never believed in mincing words.

Darling Eric,

Hold onto your hat, boy, because I've got grim news for you. The fact is, darling, I'm pregnant — and it's yours!

I learned it today when I went down to Branshoot to a local doctor's — no, he didn't know who I was, or where from.

But it creates a situation, my sweet, doesn't it? Of course it's natural for women to have babies, but as a rule it's usual for them to have husbands first.

Still, we don't have to be Victorian about it, my dear. The obvious thing to do is to get married. I'm afraid I'm too far advanced to get rid of it now, Eric, even if I knew where or how.

So it seems we'll just have to say goodbye to our schooldays and start married life together — let's just hope to God we make a go of it.

I don't want you to get all excited and upset, precious, but I think we'd better talk it over together. Therefore, I want you to come to the woods tonight.

I've heard a rumour, which I understand is true, that Joey Lodge won't rent that room at the Swill Bin anymore. Okay. We'll rub along without it. If you meet me in the garden of the Swill Bin at one o'clock — that will be the best spot. We can't miss one another then.

Don't forget, my love; give your answer to Phyll, and she'll tell me. She knows all about it.

Looking forward to seeing you, darling — goodbye until tonight — or rather, tomorrow morning, early.

Your adoring sweetheart,
Marjorie xxx

For quite a long time Baxter just sat and glared at the note, absolutely aghast. This was awful — terrible! He hardly dared think what his folks would say. And yet — there was a bright side to it.

He and Marge would have to be married. They'd leave school and be together always . . . he needn't fear that she'd fall for any other man now, for he'd be bound to her, and she to him.

Which showed how little Baxter knew about Marge's character.

After skipping one dance, Baxter went

over to Phyllis again.

He danced with her, and she said:

'You've read it?'

'Yes.' He was subdued.

'You will — you will marry her?'

'Of course. You'll deliver a message from me?'

Phyllis nodded

'Just say it'll be all right about tonight. The time and the place she mentions. I'll be there.'

'All right, Eric. I'm so sorry — '

He smiled half-heartedly, and they clapped in a desultory fashion as the dance ended.

Having attended to the note, Baxter felt he needed some air. He wandered out into the gardens surrounding the road-house, and sat on a bench by the porch. The porch light illuminated his face, and revealed it to be almost grey.

He took the note from his pocket again. For the second time he read it, and then re-read it again.

It seemed hard to believe. He'd been sure nothing like this could happen to Marge and he. After all, she'd seemed so

240

experienced for her years, and —

He grunted, absently thrust the note back into his pocket without looking at it, and stood up. He decided it might be as well for him to return to the school. Certainly he didn't care to stay at the dance with this cloud on his mind.

Baxter walked down the path, and into the road.

The second he was out of sight, a dark shadow emerged from the shelter of the porch. A cigarette glowed between its fingers. The shadow stepped forward to the bench where Baxter had been sitting.

★ ★ ★

Miss Mary Nightingale, sports and athletics mistress at Munston Girls' School, was present at the dance.

Both Prenderby and Brooks were gratified by this. It wasn't every week that Mary Nightingale found the time to attend a dance; when she did, the room seemed considerably brighter for her presence. At least, so the two North

House masters thought.

Brooks himself had long been attracted to the grey-eyed, dark-haired Munston mistress. Certainly she was a very pretty girl, not more than twenty-five, and with a remarkably well-shaped figure. She stood out alongside her contemporaries like a two-hundred bulb alongside a birthday-cake candle.

Brooks danced with her.

Not to be outdone, Prenderby strolled over for the next turn, and said, 'Miss Nightingale, how pleasant to see you here. Er — shall we?'

'I'd love to, Mr. Prenderby,' said she, standing up.

And to Prenderby's unmitigated horror, the band struck up a rumba!

The waltz he danced passably well. The quickstep he managed to get round in. The slow foxtrot, though it had him more than a trifle foozled, was a dance he was game to try. But the *rumba* . . .

And Miss Nightingale was looking at him with the look of a woman who expects to be taken into the arms of a strong man, and whirled into dreamland on the polished dance floor.

'The music's started,' she hinted.

Prenderby crimsoned.

'The fact is — '

'That you can't dance the rumba? I guessed it.'

Prenderby smiled. 'I'm awfully sorry. I must look a fool. But when it comes to a rumba, I have to hand it to younger feet — like Brooks'.'

Mary smiled. 'You don't have to hand anything to younger feet, and certainly not to Brooks.'

Prenderby felt flattered.

'I insist you dance with me,' said Mary, firmly. 'You've asked for it, and now you're not going to back out. You can at least try.'

They got onto the floor, and Prenderby spent a hapless three minutes being taught the basic step. But he was adaptable, and by the time the second encore started, he was getting round, if not well, at least without treading on the dainty dance shoes of his instructress.

The dance finished, and Mary laughed.

'You see? It's so simple. Isn't it?'

'With such a pleasant teacher,' he replied.

She flushed a little.

'Thank you, Mr. Prenderby . . . '

He said, 'I wonder if you'd care for a drink?'

She hesitated. Then murmured: 'Frankly, I find it a bit hot in here. I'd far rather take a stroll in the gardens.'

Prenderby jumped at the chance. 'Then allow me to come along with you.'

'I was hoping you would,'

They went out.

'It's wonderful out here,' mused Mary, taking Prenderby's arm in a natural fashion as he strolled beside her.

'We do have some beautiful scenery,' he agreed.

'What a pity it should be spoiled by things like that — that horrible murder in the woods last term, and — and the incident at St. Mark's. That poor little Chester man — '

Prenderby frowned. 'I still don't think he did it. Do you? I notice you said 'that *poor* little Chester man'.'

She shrugged. 'I was referring to the

fate that overtook him. It must be awful to fall in front of a train like that. I won't say he didn't deserve it, but — '

Prenderby grunted: 'I'm pretty sure he didn't.'

Miss Nightingale smiled at him, and for a few minutes they observed a silence. They felt there was no necessity to talk. This was the first time they'd been alone together, and they felt quite natural and at peace in the silence.

Suddenly, Mary said:

'Mr. Prenderby, why haven't we become friends before this?'

'But we've been friendly for some time.'

'I mean — more intimately.'

'Frankly, I've wanted to know you better, but you've always seemed so unattainable.'

'That's strange. I've felt the same way about you.'

Prenderby felt highly elated. He'd fancied that if anyone had the inside rail with Mary Nightingale, it was Brooks. This seemed to disprove that opinion.

She went on: 'Let's stop being so

formal. We've known each other for some time. Suppose you call me Mary, and I'll call you — what?'

'John,' he told her. She laughed softly, and her grip on his arm tightened.

'You think I'm a bit forward, John?'

'Hell, no — I beg your pardon — I mean, of course not. I think you're pretty wonderful — and wonderfully pretty.'

'You say some very sweet things.'

Emboldened, he murmured:

'I've been thinking them up ever since I first saw you when you came to Munston two terms ago. Never dared hope that I'd be able to repeat them to you personally, though.'

She said, 'John — it wasn't you who sent flowers and a gift anonymously, when I had my birthday at Munston last year, was it?

He smiled. 'I have to take the guilt for that, Mary.'

'That was sweet of you,' she murmured. 'I thought it might have been, at the time. But I didn't like to question you — and you never did receive any reward, did you?'

He said, 'Reward? I didn't ask for any reward. It was nothing. And my reward was the pleasure I had in doing it.'

Mary said, 'You know, lots of the girls bought me gifts. And the school porter . . . I rewarded them. All of them, John. With a — a kiss.'

Prenderby suddenly ached to take her into his arms and kiss those moist, warm, upturned lips, with a passion which had been foreign to him until now. He felt rejuvenated. Like a young man. As if this was his first woman, his first affair.

Ten minutes ago he wouldn't have believed this could happen, not even with Mary Nightingale. But now — her appealing, sweet face, her inviting lips, her soft body against him, the warm touch of her hand on his wrist . . .

Prenderby kissed her.

He kissed her with as much passion as he considered warrantable.

And Mary returned his embrace, ardently.

There was a cough behind them, and Brooks, who had wandered out in their wake, said:

'Hope I'm not interrupting anything?'

Prenderby jumped away. Mary straightened her hair. Prenderby said, 'Brooks — I ought to strangle you.'

'I wouldn't blame you,' Brooks chuckled.

15

Mr. Gregg Justifies his Suspicions

Prenderby spent the rest of that evening in a daze. How it had happened, he couldn't have said. He'd always had a warm feeling towards the lively gym mistress of Munston, but never suspected that what he felt could so easily turn into an overpowering love.

And certainly not that she could ever return his affection.

Well — for a man of his years, this was something too good to miss. Before he left Mary that night, he had arranged for a meeting the next evening, and a stroll round the countryside thereabouts.

Walking back to the school, in the wake of a horde of noisy youths, Brooks said:

'Mind if I say I think you're a lucky dog, old man?'

'I think the same myself,' agreed Prenderby. 'Still can't believe she can see anything in a frump like myself. Brooks — you don't think she's pulling my leg, do you?'

Brooks smiled. 'She isn't the type.'

'No — but I'd have expected her to have been more interested in younger men — like — well, yourself for instance.'

'I'm damned sorry she isn't. I had a sneaking hope that I might be able to — but never mind. If it hadn't to be me, then I'm glad it was you.'

'Thanks,' said Prenderby.

Brooks grinned. 'Seeing her tomorrow?'

'Probably.'

Prenderby looked at the moon, which chanced to be full — and found it extraordinarily good to look upon. Funny — he hadn't noticed what an attractive moon it was tonight. 'Nice moon, Brooks,' he said, amiably.

Brooks was mystified, 'Same old moon, old chap.'

'Hmm. But quite extraordinarily bright tonight.'

Brooks chuckled. 'That depends whose eyes are looking at it. Now looked at by the eyes of a lover — '

'Don't talk rot,' said Prenderby, flushing.

Brooks was highly amused. 'You know, I've never seen you like this before, old man. Never. Generally you're calm and cool — almost to the point of cynicism. 'Only fools and poor men get married — and I'm neither!' Didn't you say that, or something damned like it?'

Prenderby shrugged. 'I still say it.'

'You wouldn't marry Mary then?'

'Don't be a clown, Brooks. We're just good friends.'

'That kiss you exchanged didn't look platonic to me.'

Prenderby had to confess that it hadn't been platonic. 'But it didn't signify anything, you know.'

Brooks smiled broadly into the shadows, and replied: 'No, of course not.'

Prenderby still thought the moon looked extremely interesting!

★　★　★

Baxter paced up and down his study in a terrible stew. His mind tried to grasp the fact that there was actually a child on the way, that his entire future would be radically changed, and that the music had still to be faced.

He was anxious to see Marjorie. He could hardly contain himself to wait until the appointed hour.

The clock on the mantelpiece showed him the time was now almost eleven-fifty.

No sense starting out until twelve-thirty, anyhow.

They would be able to plan things out — they had to be slow and easy for a time. Their parents had to be told, and their respective schools spun some story to account for their leaving. Baxter hoped everything went off smoothly. He dreaded the idea of facing his own folks. He knew what their reactions would be.

His mother — stiff and unyielding, with a monocle, a broad personal seat, an extensive country seat, and a narrow mind. The smell of the stables always surrounding her, even indoors; due to the fact that she hardly ever bothered to wear anything other than riding habit.

He could picture the crop swishing and smacking against her corduroyed leg as he told his unhappy story.

His father —

Angular, moustached, prim, severe. Inclined to follow the lead set by his wife, who was a human dynamo when she got into her stride.

He could almost hear his mother raving

'Damnit, boy, you're a discredit to the family! You ought to be dashed well horsewhipped, eh, Horace?'

'Indeed he ought, m'dear.'

'And as for the girl — what can she be but a trollop! A veritable trollop! Eh, Horace?'

'What indeed but a trollop,' his father would agree.

'To think that this should be visited upon — ' and so on and so on, until Baxter's head was ringing with the mental voices he was conjuring up.

He said, dispiritedly, 'Hell!' and flung himself into the study armchair, where he relaxed into almost a stupor.

The one bright spot was Marge and he being man and wife. But —

He was wondering about Marjorie. Whilst the prospect of marriage hadn't been imminent, while they'd been playing a particularly intriguing game, with fruits surprisingly easy to reach, he'd been convinced that he wanted her near to him day and night, and that she wanted the same thing. But — he wondered. Looking back on their meetings and her conversation at those times, he realised that Marjorie had a very callous attitude towards life — and love.

At the time he'd brushed the idea aside, for did he not have to be sure they loved each other, to make what they were doing seem right? Hadn't he been cursed with a conscience?

But if they married, and Marge couldn't be straight —

He snapped from his reverie. The clock was striking the quarter hour. Twelve-fifteen.

He went to the bed and ferreted out his gym pumps. He began to draw them on, sitting there in the darkness.

What was that sound?

He was alert instantly. Everyone in St.

Mark's should have been in bed, asleep, by that time. Certainly no one should have been about in the Sixth Form corridor.

He went to the door soft-footedly, and paused, listening.

'Anyone there?' he said, in a hoarse whisper.

Silence.

'Must be imagining things,' he muttered, and reached out to grasp and turn the knob.

It was time to meet Marjorie.

★   ★   ★

Marjorie slid out of bed and stood shivering in her scanties and stockings. She had kept them on, ready to slip into her dress and hurry away to the meeting place.

It was a cold night, but she had no regrets that she had arranged to meet Baxter. Actually, now things had gone so far, they might have met publicly. But that didn't suit Marjorie. She wanted to see Eric alone again — and to indulge

255

herself to the full in his consternation and adoration.

Besides, she had a hope that the cold, the scramble over the rough ground, and the thrill, might possibly bring about a miscarriage. It was a forlorn hope, but if she strained herself as much as possible . . .

She began to get into her dress. Phyllis was awake. Phyllis was far more worried than Marjorie could possibly have been.

'Marge — do you think you ought to go?'

'Of course, darling. It's quite romantic, this nocturnal meeting.'

'But Marge — the woods — it isn't safe.'

'Rubbish,' laughed Marjorie, softly. 'That poor little Chester man's dead — '

'But — there's that master who prowls the woods — '

'The one called Gregg? Oh, I don't suppose I'll bump into him again, darling. Now hush — you'll be waking the dorm.'

'But Marge — wouldn't it be better if — if *I* came along?'

It was a noble offer coming from

Phyllis, who would never have dreamed of breaking bounds and entering the woods at night on her own account. But for the sake of her friend, she was willing to risk it. Marjorie's voice was very gentle when she answered:

'You're quite wonderful, Phyll. And I appreciate it, dear. But I do think you'd be a little out of place with Eric and I — we won't be talking all the time, you know.'

Phyllis said: 'I don't mind, if you'd like company — '

'Thanks, darling, but no.'

Phyllis, despite her anxiety, seemed relieved by the refusal.

'Do be careful then, Marge.'

'A great deal more careful than I've been so far,' observed Marjorie meaningfully; and with a final laugh, she tiptoed to the exit, and was gone.

Phyllis lay awake. Something told her Marjorie was going into horrible danger. She couldn't account for the feeling. Perhaps it was just her nerves, she decided at length. But still she couldn't rest. She lay awake, not even dozing, as the long minutes turned into hours, and the grey fingers of dawn stretched in at the windows and threw a pallid, sombre light upon the sleeping inhabitants of the dormitory.

She lay awake, listening anxiously for the returning movements of Marjorie.

But Marjorie never came!

★　★　★

Mr. Gregg shivered, despite the heavy greatcoat he was wearing. He turned out of the playing fields into the woods, moving silently in rubber-soled shoes. He was becoming adept at moving without making noise, in the woods.

He had told himself repeatedly that it was insane to carry on like this. And yet, he couldn't elude the suspicion that the woods still held the secret behind the death of his daughter.

Gregg had been very fond indeed of that one child of his. He had been proud and affectionate. Lavished upon her all the love he had to spare, which was a great deal. She was his only consolation for an otherwise uneventful, sometimes tragic, life. And often he had wondered how he would react if she met with an accident.

Once, in London on business, he'd seen two ambulance men carrying a sheeted figure into a hospital. The sheet had been drawn right over the head, indicating the person was dead. Seemingly the cause had been a traffic accident.

And Gregg had had a sudden fear that it might be his daughter under that sheet! He knew perfectly well she was safe in Munston at the time, but he couldn't help himself.

He had stepped forward, and said:

'Is — is it a girl?'

The stretcher-bearer had looked at him peculiarly: 'No — a young man.'

Gregg, with beads of perspiration trembling on his brow, had stepped back thankfully.

But he'd had the chance to see then how he would have reacted to any calamity which might have overtaken his daughter. He had felt, for one insufferable instant, that he was going completely insane.

That had been months before the murder.

When that had happened, he had really become demented. Not in a wild and raving manner — but he knew quite well the balance of his mentality had been destroyed, and had remained so. This obsession for scanning the woods by night proved that.

He plodded onwards, through the thickest part of the wood.

His way led in the direction of the Scarlet Rabbit. He did not walk that way consciously; after all, if he was liable to drop upon anything of interest at all, he was just as likely to find it in one place as another.

He stood in the shadow of a clump of trees opposite the rear entrance of the Scarlet Rabbit. The pub was in darkness. Clearly Mr. Lodge had retired to bed, now that his practise of admitting seniors and their girls to his back rooms had ceased.

Mr. Gregg peered keenly this way and that.

In his hand he carried a stout walking stick — more in the nature of a cudgel than a stick, really. He had not come unprepared. He was not so insane.

Unexpectedly he heard a light footfall along the path leading to the Scarlet Rabbit. He drew further back into the shadows, tensed and waiting.

He gripped his stick even tighter —

Then he snorted quietly. Coming along the path was the same girl he had warned some nights ago. He was about to step forward and confront her, angrily, when a heavy stone crashed down onto his head. The soft felt hat he wore crumpled like tissue-paper under the force of the blow. Mr. Gregg, without a cry, sank to the ground —

16

Marjorie's Worries are Ended

Marjorie didn't give a thought to the danger that there might be in the woods, as she hurried towards the meeting place. She was anxious to see Eric, and to get things settled with him. They must be married in haste; there was no time to be spared for arguments and compromises.

It was not long before she came to the clear path running to the back of the Scarlet Rabbit. The garden where she had arranged to meet Eric was reached through a small wooden gate. She had an idea he would be already there — he always was first to arrive at these meeting places of theirs.

There was a brilliant moon shining down onto the path, but where the trees made a rampart to the woods, it was shadowy.

She was almost at the gate when she

fancied she heard a slight disturbance ahead of her.

The sound came from under the trees, almost opposite the gate. She stopped, and for the first time she knew a twinge of fear.

But it was probably Eric. Of course — he was waiting for her in the shadows there.

She took a forward step.

'Eric . . . '

There was no answer. The shadows were deep, but she could distinguish a vague black shape there.

'Eric — is it you, Eric?'

The shadow was motionless. She sensed it was watching her avidly, intently. She began to feel panic.

Slowly, step by step, she backed away —

The shadow moved, and as it did so her eyes caught a flash of white near its feet, and she realised with a sudden shock that there was a man down there. Or at least, a human being.

The fear that it might be Eric came to her.

Her throat and mouth were dry. She wanted to run, to scream, but some inner power seemed to have paralysed her muscles and her vocal cords.

The shadow came towards her, and now it was revealed by the moonrays as it stepped onto the path.

Marjorie took just one look at its eyes, then her petrified muscles found the strength to let her turn and run —

Gasping and panting, she raced along the path.

The figure raced after her, with effortless ease. Marjorie turned off into the woods.

Or that was her intention. But a tree root, half-sunk below ground, was her undoing. Her feet tangled in it, and she crashed to the ground with a force that knocked the breath from her body.

She scrambled to her knees, grazed and breathless. For the first time in her life she knew a soul-searing panic and fright. The shadow of the figure loomed above her, and she screamed . . . but it was a soundless scream — her dry throat, her paralysed vocal cords, refused to give it volume.

She shrank back in terror as the figure hurled onto her —

★　★　★

'The fact of the matter is,' said Prenderby, to Brooks, as they took an early-morning shower in the Masters' Bathroom, 'that Gregg will get himself dismissed if he doesn't wake up to the realities of life and stop this prowling business. Although there may be a great deal of method in his madness — I, for one, think whoever murdered Beasly and Gregg's daughter is still at large.'

Brooks towelled himself down briskly, then threw the towel aside.

Prenderby murmured: 'Frankly, I think I can feel for Gregg. I'd feel pretty much the same now if anything happened to Mary.'

Brooks answered with a flat: 'Lucky dog.'

Prenderby yawned. 'Oh, well — brekker, I suppose,'

They went into Big Hall. The bell had

not yet gone, but Dr. Wignall liked his masters to be early at table. Also, he insisted they take their meals with the boys — no serving was allowed in their Common Room or studies.

They sat at Long Table at the head of the room, and surveyed the rabble of schoolboys pouring in to take their places.

'Jones Minor!' barked Prenderby, suddenly. 'The bread on the table is intended for the purpose of eating, and not for the purpose of throwing at Mornington's head — laudable as that purpose may seem to you.'

Jones Minor, who had not been aware that he was observed, made haste to set the bread plate down and seat himself.

Prenderby sighed. Brooks grinned.

'Now what about your free school, old man? You'd have grubby little rotters like Jones Minor pranging around.'

Prenderby smiled. 'That would be one of the snags. But I think they could be straightened out by patience and kindness rather than discipline. Besides, their own pals would boycott them if they went too far.'

A maidservant set plates of bacon and egg before them. The seniors, faced by an unappetising array of burned kippers, looked enviously and darkly at the superior fare of the Masters.

'This food discrimination is something I do not hold with,' said Prenderby. 'Damn it, if *we're* having bacon and eggs, then the school should have the same.'

'Sorry,' Brooks replied, 'my mouth's too full of bacon and egg to argue about it.'

Prenderby, despite his recent remarks, tackled the breakfast with gusto.

He was halfway through his second fried egg when the school porter came into the room and over to his side.

'You're wanted on the telephone, sir. It's that there Police Inspector that was here at the school. He says it's important.'

Brooks raised his eyes curiously. Prenderby wiped his fingers on a napkin, and got up.

'Excuse me.'

He went to his study and took the call there. The inspector's voice came through:

'Mr. Prenderby?'

'Speaking.'

The inspector said, 'I thought I'd give you a call since you've interested yourself in this business of the murders — '

Prenderby tensed. 'Go on, Inspector.'

'There's been another. Just going along to look things over now. Perhaps you'd like to come along — as it happens there's one of your fellow masters implicated.'

'*What?*'

'I believe Gregg's his name. Matter of fact, I haven't actually seen him yet. Lodge of the Scarlet Rabbit rang through a few minutes ago to say he'd found the body of a girl, mutilated badly, and an unconscious man — on the path at the rear of his pub.'

Prenderby said, 'I'll come at once,'

'I'll see you there, then.'

Prenderby hung up, then went out into the Quad and across. As he passed the side door, Brooks came out.

'Saw you haring away, from the dining-hall window,' he explained. 'Is there anything wrong?'

'A great deal, seemingly. The inspector has just been notified of another murder ... and they've found Gregg unconscious, at the scene, as far as I can gather.'

'The devil they have!' echoed Brooks.

'I'm not sure whether the Inspector called me to come along and take care of Gregg, or because he thinks I'm interested in the killings.'

'Who's been killed?' said Brooks.

'A girl, as far as I can gather.'

'A girl?'

'Didn't say whether she was a village girl, or what ... I'm getting right over there now.'

'Who found the bodies?'

'Lodge of the Scarlet Rabbit.'

'Good God! Did it happen there?'

'Apparently.'

'In the pub?'

'Far as I know, on the path at the back. That's where the bodies were found.'

Brooks hesitated, and then: 'Any objection to my coming along, Prenderby?'

'I have none. I don't know about the inspector. Still, I hardly think he'll object.'

They started out towards the boundary of the woods, across the playing fields. Despite Prenderby's advanced age he walked at a speed that caused the younger master to half-run. Puffing and blowing, Brooks toiled into the woods behind him.

'As I told them,' said Prenderby, moving with effortless strides, 'it wasn't Chester. I knew damned well it wasn't. This proves it.'

'Perhaps this time they'll get some lead on who it actually is doing these killings,' hazarded Brooks.

'Let's hope so. There doesn't seem to be any end to it.'

They were making good time through the undergrowth. Brooks had gained his second wind, and was moving comfortably now. As they came out onto the pathway, they heard the sound of a car engine up ahead.

'That will probably be the car and ambulance,' said Prenderby. 'They haven't arrived much before us, at any rate.'

They came in sight of the Scarlet Rabbit and a group of people gathered some twenty feet or so farther along, at the wood side of the pathway.

As they drew level, the inspector turned. His features were grave, his lips pursed.

'Mr. Prenderby. Good morning.'

'Good morning, Inspector.'

'Serious business this,' said the inspector, shaking his head. 'The poor kid's been put through it all right. I'd say it was the work of the same person that murdered the girl here last year.'

Prenderby pressed through the edge of the throng. He turned his face away for a moment to recover his composure, then looked down again.

Brooks, behind him, gasped: 'Ugh!'

The girl was lying on her back, her right leg outstretched, her left leg twisted under her. Her clothing was disarranged; part of it had been removed altogether, and cast away at the side of the path.

She was very badly mutilated — her face seemed to have been struck several times with a heavy object: probably the rock which was lying nearby, soaked with blood.

The inspector said to a white-faced, hand-wringing Joey Lodge: 'Do you know the girl?'

'No sir. Not me. Never seed her afore.'

Brooks chimed in: 'I think I recognise her, sir. I rather think she's one of the Munston girls — '

Prenderby peered more closely, then exclaimed: 'By Heaven, you're right too. She is. I remember seeing her at the dance once or twice. One of our boys was very keen on her — at least, he was always with her — '

'Baxter, wasn't it?' said Brooks.

'I believe it was. Yes, Baxter.'

Joey Lodge said, 'I don't know anything about it. I just came out the back door this morning for a stroll, and found these 'ere. I left them like they was, and phoned the law right away.'

The inspector nodded. 'You did right, Mr. Lodge.'

He took Prenderby by the arm, and drew him over to a knot of three constables some yards away.

'This is your man Gregg, isn't it?'

Gregg looked pale and ill. He was flat

out on a canvas stretcher, and his head was a mess of blood.

Prenderby said, 'Poor old Gregg. Yes, that's him.'

'Had a pretty bad knocking about. Seems he's been hit once or twice on the head with a rock or something. Hasn't come round at all yet. They're taking him to the hospital in the car, to get him fixed up there.'

They watched Gregg raised and lifted into the vehicle. Then they turned back to the first group.

'Have you found anything out?' asked Prenderby. 'Any clues, or anything of that nature?'

The inspector said: 'Yes. I didn't mean to show this to anyone yet, but — here, you take a look at it . . . '

He took a small envelope from his pocket, opened it, and handed a blood-stained scrap of paper to Prenderby.

Prenderby took it gingerly, and with some difficulty he was able to decipher the text of the message written there.

When he had finished reading, the inspector said: 'Well?'

Prenderby frowned. 'I — I hardly know what to think.'

'This fellow Baxter — the one you claim was always with her at the dances — his name wouldn't happen to be Eric, would it?'

'I — yes, I think it is. But Baxter wouldn't do a thing like this. You don't know him, Inspector,'

The inspector shook his head. 'Not at present, I don't. But I have a feeling I will shortly. I'll know him very well.'

Prenderby expostulated: 'But the note, even if meant for him, doesn't prove anything. It may never have been delivered. Perhaps she dropped it herself.'

'If it *hadn't* been delivered, there wouldn't have been any point in her *being here*, would there?'

'No, I dare say you're right. Then, if that note was sent to Baxter, it means — '

'That he has been here. And if he has been here — I'm afraid we'll have to hold him. It's too early to decide anything yet, but we must question Baxter as soon as we can.'

Prenderby, at the risk of cutting classes and getting a nasty lecture from Dr. Wignall, returned to the local police station with the inspector.

He was both puzzled and worried about that note which the inspector claimed to have located near the body. If Baxter had received a note of that description, the picture certainly looked black for him.

'Then there's the school that the girl belonged to,' the Inspector was saying, and Prenderby snapped out of his reverie.

'What was that, Inspector?'

'I said, I must telephone the Munston school and let them know — '

'Oh. Of course. I'm afraid Miss Scotch will be horrified.'

'Miss Scotch?'

'She is the Headmistress of Munston Girls'.'

The telephone rang. The inspector picked it up. 'Yes,' he said. 'Yes — as far as you can judge, eh? Well, it can be confirmed. Yes, of course. Thank you.'

He put down the telephone. He said:

'That was the doctor — he thinks the girl is pregnant. Or rather, was. She's been strangled, then battered, like the other.'

Prenderby said, 'Pregnant?'

'That makes it look even blacker for this Baxter of yours. The note leads one to believe that he and this girl were in the habit of hiring a room at night at the Scarlet Rabbit. That leaves the thing open to only one construction. And, as a result of those meetings, the girl obviously became pregnant. She told the boy so in the note — and he, fearing the scandal and disgrace, possibly took steps to shut her mouth!'

Prenderby was aghast.

'Good Heavens, no!' He turned to Brooks. 'Do you think Baxter capable of an act like that?'

'Of causing the girl's condition, yes,' said Brooks, judicially. 'Of killing her, certainly not.'

The inspector said, 'We have to go by the evidence . . . '

The telephone rang again, and he answered it.

He put it down. 'The hospital again. Your man Gregg has finally responded to treatment. He's conscious. Care to come along?'

They left the station together to go over to the local hospital in the inspector's car.

17

Baxter Must Worry a Good Deal!

Gregg could tell them nothing. He had been struck down. The blow had been forceful. It was likely that he would not see the outside of Munston Cottage Hospital for at least a week.

He said, sadly, as Prenderby and the Inspector prepared to leave:

'And to think I had him in my hands — if only I'd had any idea he was behind me there — '

The inspector said, when they were outside again:

'Prenderby, you can do me a favour.'

'What is that, Inspector?'

'I'm anxious to get along and see this fellow Baxter. If you'd be good enough to go along to Munston Girls' School, and break the news — I could do it by telephone, but — in view of the circumstances, and what you say of Miss

Scotch, I'd prefer it to be handled diplomatically. Will you?'

Prenderby said, 'Certainly, Inspector.'

'Thank you.'

Brooks chipped in: 'Is there anything I can do, Inspector?'

'There is nothing at present, Mr. Brooks, thank you.'

Prenderby murmured: 'Brooks, you'd better get along back to the school with the inspector. He may need some assistance there — I suspect Dr. Wignall won't be fit to give it to him once he's heard the news.'

Brooks said, 'Right-ho, old man.'

They broke up, and Prenderby wended a thoughtful way towards Munston Girls' School.

He was halfway across the yard when a cheerful-sounding voice hailed him; turning, he beheld Mary bearing down upon him from the direction of the low red-brick building which housed the gym and swimming bath.

'John — I've just been thinking about you.'

He took her outstretched hand, and

was sure again that he was in love with this pretty, clear-eyed creature.

'It's nice to see you again, Mary — when was it? Just last night? It seems a century.'

She caught a tenseness in his tone. 'This isn't a social call, though, is it?' she asked.

'No,' he confessed, 'it isn't.'

She was anxious now. 'Is something very wrong?'

'Something *is* very wrong,' he acknowledged.

'Concerning Marjorie Payne?'

'Why should you think this concerns Marjorie Payne?'

'There's a small riot on here at the moment. You see, Marjorie wasn't present at breakfast this morning, nor did she arrive in time for classes — Miss Scotch is both worried and angry. She has questioned the dormitory — and Marjorie's friend, Phyllis, who is very anxious about her chum, admitted that Marjorie had left the school late last night to meet a boyfriend from St. Mark's. She would not give the boy's name. Miss Scotch rang Dr. Wignall — he said he knew of nothing untoward, and advised her to contact the police — of course, she wishes to avoid doing so if possible. She is sending a party of the mistresses out into the woods — to look — '

Prenderby took both her hands.

'I'm afraid they'll be wasting their time, Mary. You see — the poor child is dead.'

'Dead?' Mary gasped.

'Worse, really. She was murdered, like Gregg's daughter, in the woods, last night or early this morning. I have just come from the scene of the crime . . . the inspector has asked me to break the news to Miss Scotch.'

'Oh *no* — John — ' Mary shuddered. 'You say she'd been murdered like — like Gregg's daughter?'

'The two cases are precisely similar. And, Mary — the girl was going to have a baby.'

The gym mistress found it hard to believe. She murmured:

'That will upset Miss Scotch, more than the murder itself. Oh, John — I hate to think of breaking the news to her.

Apart from the fact that she's an awful snob, she's rather a dear — and often very human indeed.'

Prenderby shrugged. 'It has to be done. And I think we had better go along now, before she has time to work herself up any more about Marjorie's absence.'

They walked across to Miss Scotch's study, slowly. Neither of them fancied the task ahead.

In answer to their tap on the door, Miss Scotch called:

'Come in, please.'

They went into the study. Three mistresses were arranged in front of the desk. Miss Scotch was addressing them commandingly.

As Mary and Prenderby entered, she waved a hand and said: 'Ah, good morning, Mr. Prenderby . . . I will not detain you a moment. One of my foolish girls — '

She faced the mistresses again.

'You understand? We must have news of her. I do not wish to contact the police — and yet she may well have run away with some man. So do not spare your efforts, ladies, and — '

Mary interrupted: 'I don't think the search will be needed, Miss Scotch. Marjorie has been found . . . Mr. Prenderby is here to tell you — tell you — '

Miss Scotch turned to Prenderby. 'You have news of the disobedient girl?' Then, noticing his serious expression, she turned to the three mistresses.

'You may go, ladies. You need not bother to search.'

Curious and speculative, they left.

Miss Scotch turned towards Prenderby again. 'Where is the girl, Mr. Prenderby, and what has she been doing? Upon my word I will see that she is expelled for last night's work . . . '

Prenderby said, quietly: 'She is in no position to be expelled, Miss Scotch. I very much fear that Miss Payne is dead.'

'D-dead?' breathed Miss Scotch.

Her fingertips crawled along the edge of the desk like five small white snakes, in her nervous and muscular reaction to this startling piece of information.

Prenderby said, 'She was killed in the woods last night.'

Miss Scotch gulped. She sank back into her chair. Her fingers continued to knead the desk edge.

After a moment of silence, she opened a desk drawer with fumbling hands, and took therefrom a half-bottle of Scotch whisky. She said, feebly: 'I must ask your indulgence whilst I — take something — for — for my heart, you know — '

'Of course,' said Prenderby.

Miss Scotch's heart was apparently in bad shape. She had almost finished what was left in the bottle before she fixed her eyes on Prenderby again.

'I feel better now,' she said. 'Kindly tell me the details of this unfortunate affair — '

Quietly, he told her the sorry story. By the time he had finished she was in a panic again. He left her muttering that this would be the ruination of her, and Munston Girls' School.

* * *

Pritchet said, 'Please sir, Mr. Brooks sent me to ask if you could come along to the study, sir.'

284

Dr. Wignall, who was taking a Sixth Form class in Latin, frowned with annoyance.

'Mr. Brooks, you say? To which study, my boy?'

'Your study, sir.'

Dr. Wignall sighed, and turned to his class.

'Baxter, you will continue the reading until I return.'

Then he left the classroom. Pritchet walked along behind him for part of the way. But as they neared the study, Wignall said, 'You need not follow, my boy. You may return to your class.'

Disappointed, Pritchet went. He had hoped to be in on the scene that was to come. He knew that Brooks would get what Pritchet called 'a jolly good jawing' for cutting classes — and Prenderby also, when he came back.

But evidently it was not to be. Pritchet returned crestfallen to his form, and Dr. Wignall, with a brow of wrath, hurried on to demand an explanation from Brooks of his absence that morning.

To his surprise, Brooks was accompanied by the Inspector of Police. They were awaiting him in his study whence the caretaker had shown them. And Brooks' demeanour, no less than that of the inspector, was so grave as to considerably dampen Wignall's flood of indignation and rebuke.

'Mr. Brooks! Where have you been, sir? And Mr. Prenderby? I will have you know that masters at St. Mark's do not abstain from their regular duties without first consul — -'

The inspector cut him off. 'I must take responsibility for drawing your two masters from their work today, Doctor.'

Wignall said, 'Really, Inspector? And are you also responsible for the absence of the third? Mr. Gregg?'

'Mr. Gregg is in hospital.'

Brooks said, kindly, 'I think you had better be seated, Dr. Wignall. What we have to tell you is not pleasant.'

Wignall argued no more. The signs were evident. There was some startling news to come. He felt he could take it better sitting down. He sat down. He took it.

When the explanation was concluded,

he was unable to find anything to say.

But at length, with a haggard face, he muttered: 'And you think — Baxter of the Sixth?'

'I think so, sir,' said the Inspector. 'But that is not for me to judge. However, I desire to question Baxter at once, with your permission.'

'Of course,' agreed Wignall. He pressed a bell, and Thomas the pageboy-cum-boots presented his polish-smeared countenance.

'Sir?'

'Will you ask Baxter of the Sixth Form to join us here?'

'Sir.'

Thomas departed. The inspector murmured: 'I may be unduly pessimistic, but I feel it likely that Baxter may attempt to escape — if he is guilty, and has any knowledge of the nature of this call. And if he is guilty, he surely must have?'

Brooks said, 'Oh, come, man. I think you're taking a bit too much for granted. I wouldn't be surprised if Baxter hadn't had anything at all to do with this horrible business.'

The inspector pursed his lips. 'That remains to be seen. In the face of the evidence, I fear that it is a view to which I cannot subscribe.'

Dr. Wignall looked up, and his features were shockingly grey.

He looked very old now.

'Do you wish to see Baxter alone, Inspector?'

The inspector shook his head. 'There is no necessity for that.'

There was a tap at the door. Dr. Wignall called: 'Come in, Baxter.'

Baxter entered. His eyes travelled to the three men slowly, as he stood just inside the door. 'You sent for me, sir?'

'I did, Baxter. The inspector has a few questions to ask you.'

'Yes, sir.'

The inspector walked round the desk and faced the Sixth Former. He wasted no time. It was his method to shock the truth from his suspects.

'You knew a girl called Marjorie Payne, I think, Baxter?'

'Why, yes sir. I met her at dances, and — and we were good friends — '

'Rather more than good friends. You knew her intimately?'

Baxter whispered, 'Yes, sir.'

'In point of fact, she was pregnant by you.'

Baxter looked down at the study floor, unable to meet the eyes of the masters. 'I suppose it had to come out sooner or later — yes, sir. I believe I am responsible for her condition. We mean to marry,' he added, belatedly.

'And yet this has been a considerable blow to you, has it not? This business of the girl. It would shock your parents?'

'I — expect so, sir. Very much.'

'It would mean the end of your schooling here?'

Wignall interrupted: '*I* can vouch for that, Inspector. I have never in all my — '

'*Please*, Dr. Wignall.'

Wignall shut up, but continued to glare sulphurously at Baxter.

That unfortunate was mystified.

The inspector continued: 'If possible, you would rather nothing concerning the child had come to light. Is that not so?'

'But it *has* to come to light,' said Baxter.

'But if the girl was unable to tell who was the father of the child she expected — '

'That's ridiculous. I'd never thought of dodging the issue.'

'She was arranging for your marriage — '

Baxter said, 'Why do you keep saying *was?* You talk of Marge as if she's — she's — ' A horrible suspicion gripped him. His voice rose to an unbelievable pitch of shrillness suddenly:

'She isn't — ?'

'Yes,' the inspector said. 'I'm afraid she is dead, Baxter.'

Baxter said, 'Christ,' and blubbered like a child.

Brooks glanced at him sympathetically. His look at the inspector said, Take it easy with him —

But that was by no means the inspector's intention. Baxter was emotionally off-guard, and ripe for questioning . . .

'Now, my boy,' said the inspector, less

harshly. He was not wholly convinced that the show of emotion was genuine — he had seen many good actors in the dock before that day. But in case it was no fraud, and Baxter was really feeling the thing so deeply, he softened his tone. 'I must ask you some questions concerning your movements last night.'

Baxter looked up. The spasm of weakness was over temporarily. He was suffering from shock, and looked and felt dazed.

'You received a note from Miss Payne last night — '

'No — yes. Yes, I did.'

'Delivered to you by hand?'

'Her friend gave it to me at the dance. But — I can't produce it now. I've lost it. Was — was Marjorie — was she murdered?'

The inspector said, 'Yes, she was murdered. In the woods, like the other.'

'God!'

'It seems strange that you didn't know, when you met her there last night.'

'But that's the point. I — didn't meet her.'

'You mean you ignored her note?'

'Yes. No — I mean — I couldn't help it. I — meant to go. Of course I meant to go — I wanted to marry her — I loved her. But — when I was ready to leave, I found my study door locked!'

Brooks raised his eyebrows.

'I was not aware that there were keys to the Sixth Form studies?'

The inspector checked him sharply. 'I will do the questioning, thank you, Brooks. Baxter — is it true that there are no keys to your study?'

'Well — yes sir.'

'And yet you found the door locked?'

'Yes, sir.

'Then how could that be? Do you imply that some person locked it, after you had entered your room?'

'I thought some of the chaps might he having a rag, sir.'

'Yet you had this appointment, and did not raise a disturbance so you would be released?'

'I could not have given any explanation for wishing to leave my study so late at night.'

'You could have given a — natural one, Baxter.'

'Oh — I didn't think of that.'

'If what you state is correct, you must have got someone to release you this morning when you woke?'

Baxter was confused. 'Well — no — you see ... well, the door wasn't locked when I woke this morning.'

'Was *not* locked?'

'No. I — took it for granted the same chap who'd locked me in had unlocked the door again.'

'It seems rather a senseless joke to me.'

'It did to me, sir.'

'And how did the person procure a key, when there are no keys?'

Dr. Wignall put in: 'There is a set of master keys that hang in the porter's lodge, Inspector. One of those unlocks all the doors on the Sixth Form corridor.'

The inspector said, 'I see. Brooks — would you do me the favour of slipping along to the porter's lodge, and bringing those keys here?'

'Certainly.'

'Kindly ask the porter to come as well,'

Brooks went out. Baxter faced the music again.

'The note this young lady sent to you. You say you lost it?'

'Yes sir.'

'Where?'

'Somewhere between the roadhouse and the school.'

'When?'

'Last night.'

The inspector looked at Dr. Wignall. Then he shook his head and came back to Baxter again.

'Let me suggest to you that in your panic at learning that this girl was to bear your child, and the fear of disgrace which that would inevitably bring, you crept out to the meeting place appointed, and hid in wait there. You were disturbed by one of your masters coming along — Mr. Gregg — and you struck him down to the ground. Then the arrival of the girl distracted your attention from him, and you savaged her and then killed her! To conceal your own misdemeanour. But for the note — *which was found at the scene of the crime, Baxter!* — suspicion would not have fallen upon you so heavily. The note suggests you were the only one to know she would be there — that you dropped it in your haste to get away once the deed had been committed . . . and that your explanation of the study door being locked is just a ruse.'

'No — '

'I'm afraid I must ask you to come to the station, Baxter.'

Dr. Wignall fanned himself weakly with a sheaf of examination papers. 'The scandal!' he muttered, brokenly.

Baxter stood firm at last. He spoke quietly, controlled now.

'Do as you think fit, sir,' he said. 'I have only one thing to say: I did not murder Marjorie. I loved her, and I wanted to marry her. I — I — this has been a terrible shock to me, and my explanations may not have been convincing. But — if you think it was me, then your duty is to take me in.'

'I'm glad you see it so sensibly. We'll make no final move until we know about the keys.'

'Very well, sir.'

Brooks came back in a few minutes, with the porter-handyman.

'Is the key missing?'

Brooks shook his head. 'No sir, it is here. You can see the marking on the loop — West Passage Number Two. That is the Sixth Form passage.'

He held up the key-ring, and exhibited the key in question,

The porter said, 'Wot's more, I'll warrant that key's been there without bein' touched for the larst ten year!'

'You are sure no one could have purloined it?'

'Well — I can't say as 'ow they couldn't 'ave. It might have been took — anytime.'

'Then had it been taken, could the thief have returned it to the ring between the hours of about two this morning and this moment?'

'That I do know they *couldn't* 'ave done. I keeps all my doors and windows tight locked, an' since I got up, there 'asn't been nobody at the lodge.'

'Your lodge is near the gates? The isolated one?'

'Yessir.'

'And you can swear this key was not replaced at any time today?'

'I can that, sir. You see, arfter I locks the gates at night with that there big key, I takes the ring into me bedroom with me, ready to 'ave 'andy like for unlockin' the gates in the mornin' . . . '

'Did you notice if the key was on the ring at any time today?'

'Never entered me 'ead. Didn't know wot all the fuss was about until Mister Brooks arsked for me keys, and told me I was to come along wif 'im.'

The inspector nodded.

'That is all. You may go, for the moment.'

The porter went. Three pairs of eyes turned upon Baxter. Three minds realised how dark was the evidence against him.

Baxter stood there, unflinching now.

'You all think I'm guilty — all right. I expect everyone else will think the same.'

There was a knock at the door. The Head said, 'Who is that?'

'Mr. Prenderby, sir.'

'Come in, Mr. Prenderby.'

Prenderby came in. His eyes took in

the scene. His brow wrinkled. He said:

'I trust Baxter has been able to clear himself?'

Brooks shook his head.

'I'm afraid he looks guilty as he — er — sin, old man.'

Baxter looked at Mr. Prenderby. His gaze was level. 'I swear I know nothing about it, sir.'

Prenderby stared into his eyes for a moment. Then he said, quietly, 'I believe that statement, Baxter,'

The inspector snorted. 'You haven't heard the results of the questioning.'

'My opinion will be the same, even so.'

The inspector grunted, 'Well, I shall have to take the boy along. He's quite of age to face things like this. I won't make any definite report to the papers for the moment. You may have a bigger bug than me on this case yet; probably someone from the Yard. It depends whether we call them in — personally I doubt if it's necessary. I think we have the culprit.'

Prenderby said, quietly: 'It is not your place to condemn, Inspector.'

He walked to Baxter. Gripped his

hand. He said, 'Chin up, my boy. Anyone who knows you well couldn't possibly think you'd kill a person. I'll do my best to help you in any way I can.'

Baxter replied quietly: 'Thank you, sir. Goodbye.'

And the Inspector took him away —

18

Dr. Wignall is Very Weary

The school buzzed with the amazing denouement of the woods affair.

Baxter taken away — detained at the station until a warrant was issued, then put in the cells!

It was incredible — Dr. Wignall, it was said, was prostrate, ministered to by his capable wife.

Mr. Prenderby openly asserted that he believed Baxter entirely innocent. But the majority of the school wondered. After all, it was the fact that the girl had been carrying Baxter's child that made things look so black. Then again, Baxter's explanation about his locked door was feeble.

Brooks said to Prenderby: 'Honestly, old man, *don't* you think he's guilty? Or are you just being stubborn?'

Said Prenderby: 'How about poor old Chester?'

'Chester?'

'The same. They were all ready to blame him — he was the scapegoat not long ago. But this proves he didn't have anything to do with Beasly's murder, doesn't it?'

'Oh, no,' said Markham, joining them. 'I don't agree there, Prenderby. Damn it all, there's no proof that the murders are connected in any way.'

'Some people can't see beyond the end of their long noses,' snorted Prenderby, who felt very strongly on the subject. 'Markham, you knew Baxter fairly well — '

'We all did.'

'Would you be willing to believe that he had murder in his soul? Cold, deliberate, cruel murder?'

'No — but I wouldn't have said the young rogue could be meeting and seducing a schoolgirl at night in a low pub, either.'

Brooks chuckled. 'He's made a point, old man.'

Prenderby grunted, and said no more. But he himself was convinced of Baxter's innocence, as he had been convinced of Chester's.

Late that same night, the inspector called.

He came to see Prenderby, and the latter took him to the solitude of his study.

'Came along to see what the reaction to Baxter's arrest has been,' said the Inspector, filling his pipe from the pouch Prenderby offered. 'Thanks.'

Prenderby lit up, and dragged hard. He got the pipe drawing to his satisfaction.

'What reaction did you expect?'

'I don't exactly know. I had an idea they'd all be amused at the turn of events.'

'They aren't. I'm afraid that fully three-fifths of them are prepared to believe Baxter actually was the killer.'

The inspector frowned.

Prenderby said, 'Just as in Chester's case, you're not too satisfied with Baxter's arrest, are you?'

The inspector leaned forward confidentially. He said:

'I'll speak freely — not as an official, but as a man. I'm off-duty, Prenderby, and any remarks I make are off the record, you understand.'

'Of course.'

'Then, between us two, I do not think Baxter is guilty.'

'You took him, though.'

'I hated to do it. But I have to think of my duty. It makes no difference what I choose to think. None. What I think is not evidence, Prenderby. And I have to act on evidence.'

Prenderby was silent for a few moments. Then:

'What'll happen to Baxter if the real culprit isn't found? And if nothing fresh is brought to light in his favour?'

The inspector was very grave. After a while, he said:

'You know, Prenderby — he'll hang.'

'They won't send a schoolboy to the gallows?' Prenderby was aghast.

'If he's judged guilty. The circumstances — '

'The devil with circumstances! He's just a boy.'

'Not a boy — a man. There are youths of his age in the world who've been earning their own livelihoods for years. Just because he happens to be attending school doesn't make any difference in the eyes of the law and the jury. He committed a despicable action in getting a schoolgirl into trouble. Then, instead of doing the right thing, he killed her to hide his own guilt. That's how they're sure to look at it.'

Prenderby's pipe had gone out. He sucked morosely at the stem.

'There must be something we can do.'

'It hinges on that key. I'm having it tested for fingerprints — '

'And — ?'

'If strange prints are found on it, that will be a point in Baxter's favour.'

Prenderby grunted. 'Not much hope of that. This killer is too clever not to wipe the key . . . '

'You're right. If there really is someone else behind all this, he's an extraordinarily cunning person.'

'Are you of the opinion that whoever committed this crime was also guilty of the death of Gregg's daughter, and of Beasly?'

The inspector scratched his head thoughtfully.

'I wouldn't care to swear to that. There have been a lot of these killings up and down the country recently. For example, about eight months ago, a young girl undergraduate was murdered by a sex slayer in the Oxford district. That case had similar points. A few weeks after that, there was a repeat of the murder with another victim. Then things quietened down at Oxford . . . and started here. There was Gregg's daughter . . . and, a few weeks ago, a horrible murder at Brighton. A young woman found on the seashore, dreadfully mutilated. Sex slayer again . . . '

'It's devilish,' said Prenderby.

'It is. We haven't got the guilty chaps in those cases. But if we started linking murders together, we could damn near pin them all on one murderer. It would cramp us — so you see, we like to keep each case separate, until we know for sure that one man committed two or more of the killings.'

'Will it help Baxter if he can provide an

alibi for the time Gregg's daughter was murdered?'

'I'm afraid it won't. He'll be tried for *this* murder, not for that one. That will not enter into the case, either for prosecution or defence.'

Prenderby laid his pipe aside and shook his head.

'There must be some clue somewhere as to the real killer. You chaps are fond of saying every murderer makes some slip.'

'We aren't fond of saying that at all. Novelists are — we know there are many criminals who make *no* slip. This looks like one of those cases.'

He stood up and took his hat.

'I'll keep you informed, Prenderby. And — if you find out anything, let me know, will you?'

'I will. You might give Baxter my best wishes — tell him I'll be along to see him tomorrow.'

'He's taking it very well,' observed the inspector. 'Though God knows, he's damned upset about the girl. You can see that. It's one of the things that helps convince me he's innocent. I know acting when I see it. That boy isn't acting. He doesn't seem to care much what becomes of him.'

After he had gone, Prenderby sat down with his pipe for company, and thought long and hard. There was a clue to the mess somewhere — something that someone had said or done. He knew there was something — if he could only remember exactly what it was that lurked, worrying him, in a dark corner of his mind, he felt he could piece the jigsaw together . . . but when he went to bed later, he was still no nearer the answer.

* * *

Pritchet said:

'Hmm. Oh, well — Baxter's had his fun, and now he'll have to pay for it. Frightful chump — fancy doing the girl in. I mean, *she* must have been an idiot too. There's ways of getting rid of brats that aren't wanted.'

'What do you know about it, Pritch?' grunted Grass.

Pritchet winked meaningfully.

'More than you'd think, old man.'

'You haven't had to persuade anyone to get rid of one, have you?' demanded Grass.

'Haven't I, though.'

Grass snorted.

'You're just acting big again.'

'That's what you think! I can jolly well tell you — '

'Rot!' snapped Grass.

Pritchet produced a pencil, and began to execute a crude design on the wall of the lavatory against which they were leaning.

Grass looked at it, said, 'You *are* a dirty skunk, Pritch.'

Underneath the design Pritchet wrote, in bold letters:

FROM JOHN PRENDERBY — FOR
MARY NIGHTINGALE.

Grass said, curiously: 'Mary Nightingale?'

'Haven't you heard the rumour? Prenderby's gone soft on this Nightingale female. She's gym mistress at Munston.'

'I don't believe it. Prenny's darned near an old man.'

'That's when they're worst,' chuckled Pritchet.

And then, the laugh froze on his lips, as did the smile on his face. He went white. So did Grass.

Mr. Prenderby had approached quietly.

Possibly he had even overheard their conversation. But, what was worse, his eyes were fixed upon the coarse design on the wall which Pritchet had executed.

He raised his eyebrows.

'Is this *your* work, Pritchet?'

'I — I — '

'I presume that it is. And it refers to myself and a lady.'

'I — I — '

'May I ask what it is, Pritchet?'

Pritchet almost turned purple. Grass shuddered.

Mr. Prenderby shook his head gravely.

'Pritchet, I am truly sorry for you. You appear to have sunk to hitherto unsounded depths of depravity. Do *you* think it is a *very* smart thing to execute designs of this nature, and link them with the names of persons who have never done you any harm?'

Pritchet mumbled, 'I — I'm sorry, sir.'

Prenderby looked him in the eyes. Then he said:

'Pritchet, I am going to turn my back for two minutes by my watch — when I turn round again, I shall expect that little work of art of yours to have been obliterated.'

He turned sharply away.

Pritchet bent down in mental anguish and grabbed handfuls of grass. He scrubbed vigorously at the offending marks, hissing to Grass:

'Give us a hand, you ass.'

Grass pitched in with a will.

When Prenderby turned again, there was just a smeary mess on the wall: a mess of green sap and blurred lines.

Pritchet gazed at his master in fear and foreboding. But Mr. Prenderby was strangely calm. He said, quietly:

'An offence such as you have committed with your obscenities should be punishable by expulsion. If not worse — you know that, Pritchet?'

Pritchet shook like an aspen leaf.

'Ye-ye-yes, sir. I'm — I'm sorry.'

'And well you should be, Pritchet. If I did as I should, I would at once take you to your Headmaster for immediate expulsion, plus a note to your parents to explain why you were turfed out of the school — at most public schools you would also be flogged unmercifully prior to expulsion. But — '

Prenderby paused.

Pritchet brightened visibly. It seemed he was not to be marched ignominiously to his Headmaster, and expelled from the school in dire disgrace.

'Pritchet,' said Prenderby thoughtfully, 'I shall forget exactly what I saw on that wall. You will do me five hundred lines, Pritchet, for making marks on the wall. You will also be caned severely for the offence.'

Pritchet looked dismal again. To be caned by the brawny arms of Mr. Prenderby was no laughing matter. He glanced lugubriously at Grass, who was in a cold sweat as he awaited his punishment.

Prenderby said, 'You will follow me, Pritchet.'

It seemed Grass was to escape scot-free. He scuttled away, heaving sighs of relief.

Pritchet, with a feeling of foreboding, followed his housemaster.

To Prenderby's study —

And Prenderby's stout ashplant.

And Prenderby's chair, over which miscreants bent from time to time.

'Flogging has been abolished at St. Mark's,' stated Mr. Prenderby, weighing the ashplant. 'Caning has not. Personally, I am not in favour of any form of corporal punishment, but I cannot help but feel that there are times when it is warranted. And should I ever behold any more of your artwork adorning the walls, my lad — well, I had better not. Bend over, Pritchet.'

'Yes sir,' groaned Pritchet. He bent over.

Prenderby administered three hearty strokes of the ashplant, with a muscular arm which had once hauled on an oar for Cambridge.

Pritchet held his silence — with an effort.

He had expected six — even expected Prenderby to overstep the usual mark, and let him have a round dozen.

But after the three strokes, the North House master threw aside the cane, and said:

'You may go, Pritchet. And remember — a word to the wise is sufficient.'

Pritchet, smarting but thankful, went to the door. And there he turned round.

'Sir — '

'Yes?'

'I didn't think when I drew on that wall, sir — I'm sorry I acted foolishly — I — well, I'm genuinely sorry . . . and . . . and thank you for dealing with me so leniently.'

Prenderby nodded, gravely. 'You have been fortunate. You may go now.'

Pritchet went. Once he was through the door, Prenderby pursed his lips and shook his head. To himself, he muttered:

'Yes — a few like Pritchet at my 'Free' School — I'd be batting on a very sticky wicket!'

★ ★ ★

'It's shocking,' said Mills Major that evening, in the Senior Common Room. 'That's what it is, shocking.'

'Eh?' said Rake.

The seniors had been talking about the Inter-Schools Boxing Championships which were destined to take place shortly. From Mills there had been not a murmur. He had clearly been deeply immersed in his own inscrutable thoughts.

Mills Major gestured expansively.

'This business of poor old Baxter,' he said.

Rake regarded him with surprise. 'Didn't know you cared so much about Baxter.'

'Baxter? No, I don't — but that damned inspector had no right to march him away like that. Good God, man, don't you see how awful it'll be if he's convicted and — hanged!'

The others nodded.

'It'll mean we'll lose our finest cricketer, finest footballer, best runner — greatest senior cruiserweight . . . it's terrible!'

Rake grinned. The reason for Mills' worried frown was now obvious. Mills was concerned about the sporting side of the schools' activities!

Rake said, 'I thought you couldn't have got so emotional about Baxter all of a sudden.'

'Baxter? Who cares about Baxter — if he killed the kid, he deserves what's coming to him. But damn it, couldn't he have at least waited until the match with Fairleigh was over? He must have known the match depended on him.'

'Thoughtless of him,' said Rake, sarcastically. 'He had no right to hop round murdering people until we had that match in the bag, eh?'

Jones of the Sixth murmured: 'If you want my opinion, the sooner that cad gets what's coming to him, the better. Where the devil does a rotten old match enter into it?'

Mills regarded him rather as he would a blasphemer. As if at any moment he expected Jones to be struck down by some heavenly power.

Jones, however, remained on his feet.

'And in my mind there isn't any question that he did it,' he said. 'It's the quiet ones who're the deepest cads. Look at those filthy midnight meetings of his — that came out — and not before time . . . '

Rake grinned. Said, 'Yes — he was a lucky dog in one way.'

Jones sniffed. He was entirely moral, was Jones. A man of dignity and principle. Upright and honest. The typical (as Rake often remarked with a sneer) conception of a British Public School man.

Bagley of the Sixth interrupted:

'You're all a bunch of idiots. I fancy I knew old Eric better than any one of you. He couldn't have done this thing . . . Now, if it had been *Rake* — '

'You cheeky cad!' said Rake.

' — or even Mills — '

'Go and eat coke.'

' — I'd have said that the charge was justified. But not old Eric — '

Rake said, 'I saw his folks going across the Quad to old Prenny's study.'

'Father and mother?'

'Yes. Remembered them from last

Sports Day. She was dressed in tweeds and smelled of horse, and the old man was wearing morning suit and spats. She was holding forth at the top pitch of her lungs, and the old boy was nodding and saying 'Yes, m'dear', and 'No, m'dear'.'

'Must have been one hell of a shock for them,' Mills murmured.

'I expect so. And I daresay they'll let old Wignall know about it. I don't envy Wiggy his job this afternoon!'

Wignall was feeling that way himself.

Baxter's parents had borne down on him in his study in answer to the telephone message they had received. They had wasted no time, and had been travelling overnight. They were not in a sunny temper.

'Now sir,' said Mrs. Baxter, when they were comfortably seated. 'I demand an explanation. Eh, Horace?'

'Yes, m'dear,' said her husband, primly.

'My dear Mrs. Baxter — ' began Dr. Wignall.

'As Headmaster of this establishment, surely it is your duty to guard against such eventualities as this?' boomed Mrs. Baxter, getting into her stride without delay, and grinding this particular male worm underfoot. 'Eh, Horace?'

'Indeed, m'dear. He should guard ag — '

'Madam — ' expostulated Dr. Wignall.

'I had little thought when we made our decision to send our son to St. Mark's, that he would be subjected to the machinations of a scheming little trollop — a common village wench — a — '

'Marjorie Payne was not a 'village wench'. She was, in fact, a pupil at Munston Girls' School. She came of an extremely good family,' Dr. Wignall managed to get in.

'Good family or not, what could she have been but a little trollop?'

Horace Baxter said, nervously. 'Hush, m'dear. After all, the girl is dead, whatever she may have — '

'Silence, Horace.'

'Yes, m'dear.'

'Don't you think your son was equally guilty where this alliance was concerned? He is, when all is said and done, a young man — '

'Had I sent him to some other school, there would not have been these pitfalls for him. This disreputable pub — '

'I did not specifically place that public house where it is,' said Wignall, stiffly, smarting from a sense of injustice.

' — and this morally lax girls' school — '

'There would have been other pitfalls. There are pitfalls everywhere for those who are inclined to fall.'

'Bah,' snorted Mrs. Baxter. 'Eh, Horace?'

'Yes, m'dear.'

'You, sir, have failed in a paramount duty towards my son as a scholar. Your guidance has been at fault. You have deliberately — '

'Be careful, madam,' warned Dr. Wignall, flushing.

'I say you have deliberately ignored this business of the public house in the woods.'

'I knew nothing about it, until this incident took place. But since we are being vituperative, has this not struck you — the injury your boy has done the school and its name by indulging his desires in this way, and then murdering the victim of his affections?'

Mrs. Baxter felt that this was beyond the pale. She had to quell this fool, and at once. To that end, she forked into the pocket of her tweed jacket and donned her monocle.

Through this she surveyed Wignall, as if he was some minute and disgusting animalcule being observed through a high-powered microscope.

That monocle had never yet failed to conquer. It was used on acquaintances and servants alike with devastating effect.

And it completely floored Dr. Wignall.

Said Mrs. Baxter:

'Your stewardship of my son has been inefficient, Dr. Wignall. I regret ever having placed him in the midst of so much temptation. He is, after all, just a child.'

Wignall didn't answer. Faced by that glittering glass he couldn't. He was transfixed. It was like an evil eye glaring at him.

Horace Baxter surveyed him with

sympathy. He knew the power his wife could wield by simply adjusting her glass.

Dr. Wignall muttered hastily:

'You will want to see your son — '

'That is why we came. And to see if this business could not be kept quiet — '

'That is for the authorities to decide,' said Wignall. 'All I can do is express my profound regret that this unhappy incident should have occurred.'

He had intended to make allowances for the unfortunate parents. But Mrs. Baxter was not a woman one could make any allowances for. Her entire attitude destroyed sympathy. She was distressed . . . but not so much by the threat of a murder trial for her son, as by the scandal and publicity which would result from that trial.

Dr. Wignall had had enough. He said:

'Mr. Prenderby will take you along to the police station at which your son is imprisoned.'

He rang a desk bell, and the page appeared, having been awaiting the call.

He went to find Prenderby as directed,

and that worthy arrived at the study in record time.

'Mr. Prenderby, I don't believe you have met Baxter's parents. Mrs. Baxter — our North House Master, Mr. Prenderby. Mr. Baxter — Mr. Prenderby.'

Mrs. Baxter snapped:

'I think we may dispense with formalities. You are to take us to see Eric, Mr. Prenderby?'

Prenderby nodded.

'Then may I suggest that we hurry? My husband and I have not a great deal of time to spare. Horace wishes to go to London to have a confidential consultation with his lawyer. I must see police officials on the matter of hushing up the affair.'

'I am quite ready, madam,' said Prenderby.

They took their leave of Dr. Wignall. When they had gone Mrs. Wignall appeared in the study, and handed the Headmaster an extremely strong cup of tea.

Dr. Wignall murmured: 'Thank you, my dear. I need this.'

'I had a feeling you would,' said Mrs. Wignall. 'She was a somewhat overpowering woman. I remember her from her previous visit.'

'Hmm, I feel quite sorry for Mr. Prenderby.'

Mrs. Wignall murmured: 'What had she to say, dear?'

'A great deal — but she seemed to be more upset by the question of scandal than by the fact that her son faces the gallows.'

Mrs. Wignall sighed. 'I felt she would be like that. Such women don't deserve children — and those who want them are unable to have them.'

Dr. Wignall took her hand, and patted it. An action that would have surprised his scholars, had they witnessed it, for they believed him incapable of any human emotions.

'Nevertheless, we have been very happy, my dear,'

'Yes, Sam,' she said softly, 'we have been happy!'

'And will continue to be so,' he told her. 'This has finished me, Clara.

Completely finished me, as far as the school is concerned. I am too old to be subjected to events of this nature. Clara — I'm thinking of retiring . . . '

Her eyes shone.

'Oh, Sam, that would be grand — '

'Nothing to do but laze, fish, and play golf — and in the evenings a little quiet reading. No classes — no troublesome boys — no even more troublesome parents.'

'But I thought the school was your life?'

Dr. Wignall winced.

'It was — it was. But — the good name I've built up — It will be torn down — wrecked, by this — this exposure. Can you not see the Sunday newspapers? 'College Boys Hire Secret Place of Rendezvous in Woods for Immoral Purposes' — 'St. Mark's Boy Accused of Murdering Pregnant Schoolgirl' — no, my dear. After this, the school must chart a new course — with Prenderby at the helm!'

19

Mrs. Baxter is Not Sympathetic

Prenderby had a taxi waiting outside the school, and at once they began the journey.

For the first mile or so, Mrs. Baxter, still smelling strongly of a mixture of horse and Jockey Club perfume, held forth.

'I find that *you* are not without blame in this matter,' she hooted, eyeing Prenderby piercingly. 'As my son's housemaster, you must surely have had some suspicions of his nocturnal activities . . . '

'Really, Mrs. Baxter — '

'And have put an end to them,' continued Mrs. Baxter. 'Now you see whence they have led? Eh, Horace?'

'Where they have led indeed, m'dear,' agreed Horace.

Mr. Prenderby said, 'Madam, I can

sympathise with you on the score of your son's arrest, but — don't you think Baxter is old enough to know right from wrong?'

'He obviously didn't,' boomed Mrs. Baxter.

'Are you sure of that?'

'Good God,' said Mrs. Baxter, staring. 'You are not suggesting that what he did was *right*?'

'Let me make it plain that I do not consider your son to be guilty. I had thought you would know him better than to think he is — '

'How should I, when I see him only occasionally during holidays? I am not close to my son, Mr. Prenderby.'

'Of that I am aware,' nodded Prenderby. 'But is it so wrong for a grown youth to feel natural inclinations? The more so if he is in love with a young woman?'

'Young woman? A schoolgirl!'

'Not at all. A young woman.'

'You condone his conduct?'

'No — you mistake me. I do not condone it. Nor do I condemn it. It is a

pity that his control was not stronger
— but is not what your son did the
purpose of life?'

'Gad!' said Horace Baxter. 'Dashed if
he isn't right, m'dear. When you look at it
in that — '

'Silence, Horace!'

'Oh — mmm — yes, m'dear.'

Mrs. Baxter fitted her monocle, prepa-
ratory to bringing the evil eye to bear
upon this man who dared express such
perverse, unmoral views.

'You are a schoolmaster at St. Mark's?'
she said.

Mr. Prenderby said, with ease, 'I am.'

'Employed to teach the young persons
in your charge the rights and wrongs of
life?'

'Not at all. Employed to blast a little
knowledge into their skulls. It is not my
job to mould them — just to teach them.
Their parents, and the boys themselves,
will form their moral codes — irrespective
of anything I say or do.'

'Boys cannot be allowed to form their
own codes.'

'That is where I disagree.'

'I always brought Eric up to be strictly honourable — '

'And has he not been so?'

'This girl — '

'Is that a point of honour?'

She turned the full, dominating force of her eyeglass on him.

But Prenderby, to her surprise, remained unquelled. Indeed, he faced her with surprising tranquillity, and said, calmly:

'There is nothing wrong with your son, morally or honourably. In my opinion, he has been unfortunate enough to have conceived a love for a girl which does not usually come to one so young. I feel that is the truth — and I will not condemn him for giving way to that love.'

'Pshaw!' snorted Mrs. Baxter.

She would have liked to have had a horsewhip to crack at her leg. That might have helped the power of her monocle, but unfortunately she had not. Prenderby remained unmoved.

Mr. Baxter said, 'Then you do not think our son is guilty?'

'I do not. Do you?'

There was a slight hesitation. Then: 'No, I do not. And I am glad you are in accord with me, Mr. Prenderby. From what I have heard, the evidence is — '

Mrs. Baxter interrupted:

'This is pointless. The law will decide whether or not he has committed this murder. Nothing we can say or do will alter that decision.'

'Your testimony will weigh a great deal at the trial.'

'I shall not attend the trial, if I can possibly avoid it.'

'I see.'

'If Eric has killed the girl, he must pay the penalty. English law, Mr. Prenderby, is just. Eric will receive a fair trial, I have no doubt.'

'Mistakes are made — '

'But seldom — '

'There was the case of one of the masters here — Chester. He was hounded for something he did not do. I am sure of it. Now he is dead — '

'An isolated case.'

'Your son could be another such isolated case.'

Mrs. Baxter said, 'I am willing to abide by the findings in a court of law. I have lived by the law — and, if found guilty, my son can die by it!'

This callous attitude disturbed Prenderby. He felt there were too many parents without use for their children. He said:

'Have you no sympathy for the boy?'

Mrs. Baxter rejoined tartly:

'Has he no sympathy for his family? Aside of the charge of murder, had he no thought for the decent, respectable people who are his father and mother? If so, why did he risk bringing disgrace upon us — '

It was getting too much like a scene from a Victorian melodrama for Prenderby's liking.

'The boy is very upset — as is only natural. I hope that you will not be harsh with him.'

'I shall speak my mind to him,' she said. 'He is old enough to be spoken to frankly. His actions have proved that.'

Prenderby grunted, and said no more. But he had a feeling that this visit to

Baxter was not going to bring that unfortunate much consolation in his present unpleasant predicament.

The ancient taxi chugged on towards its destination.

At length the police station at Branshoot came into sight.

★ ★ ★

'In short,' said Mrs. Baxter, determinedly, 'I must insist that you keep this matter quiet, Inspector.'

The inspector glanced at Prenderby with a weary expression which as much as said: Why the devil did you wish this onto me?

But he replied:

'It *will* be kept quiet for the moment. But if your son has to face trial — and, by all the signs he will have to do so — I doubt very much whether the case can be heard in camera, or even whether your son's name can be kept a secret. If he is found guilty, there is no possibility of hushing things up.'

Mrs. Baxter said, 'I shall speak to the

Home Secretary — he is a personal friend of my brother's.'

'I fear it would make no difference if he was a brother of your own. He would still, be powerless.'

Then, before she could speak again, he pressed on:

'Your son is aware that you are here. Will you see him now?'

She nodded.

'Tonight he will be removed to Exeter Prison, later to London. This is his last day here — I would advise you to be calm, and not to show any fear or panic.'

Mrs. Baxter withered him with a broadside from her monocle.

'I trust I have complete control of myself,' she sniffed.

The inspector led them behind the desk, and along a narrow corridor, distempered green.

At the far end was a wooden door. He opened this, and they passed inside.

Baxter was seated on a rickety bench. His head was in his hands, but as the inspector said, 'Your mother is here,

Baxter,' he snapped out of his dismal reverie.

'Oh — hello, Mother. Dad — '

'Hello, my boy,' said Horace Baxter.

There was an awkward silence, during which his mother gave him the full benefit of her monocle.

The inspector said, 'Well — I — I'll leave you alone.'

He beckoned to Prenderby and they went out.

In the passage, he said: 'God help him, with a mother like that.'

Prenderby said, 'I couldn't agree more. Er — I think I'll hang on in the passage here, Inspector. I'd rather like a word with the lad, after they are finished. If you haven't any objections?'

'None. Help yourself.'

The inspector returned to the main room.

After a while, voices sounded from behind the cell door. Topmost in carrying power was Mrs. Baxter's. Prenderby could picture the monocle being brought into full play.

She was saying:

'That you could do such a despicable thing — are you ashamed of yourself?'

Baxter said, quietly: 'No.'

'What? This — this affair — this trollop of a girl you — '

Baxter cut her short. 'Marjorie was a wonderful girl. What do *you* know about her, Mother? You hadn't even met her.'

'Pah. Eh, Horace?'

There was no answer.

Mrs. Baxter went on: 'Eric, your behaviour has been abominable. Abominable. Are you not sorry, now that you see where your intrigue has led you?'

Baxter spoke quietly but firmly. This was the first time he had found courage to face up to his mother.

'I'm not sorry. I'm sorry that poor Marge has been — has been — killed. But I'm not sorry I loved her. I'm not sorry we took what that love had to offer. I'm not so — '

'Enough!' hissed Mrs. Baxter. 'You are impossible. But we must stand by you. Your father will see that you have a good defending counsel. I will see what may be done to keep this sorry affair out of the newspapers. But if you are acquitted, I wish you to understand plainly that you are not wanted at your home. You will never return there, and you need expect no financial help from us. Eh, Horace?'

'Well, my dear, I — '

'And,' hooted Mrs. Baxter, 'I mean that! You have, by your careless and immoral conduct, brought a black disgrace upon yourself and those nearest you. I will not tolerate you as a son of mine any longer. We disown you. If you are freed of the charge, you can henceforth make your own way in the world.'

Baxter said, 'I intend to do so.'

Mrs. Baxter said, 'That is all I have to say.'

She swept to the door and opened it, and Prenderby removed his ear from the woodwork just in time.

She swept into the passage.

Horace Baxter half-turned towards his son.

Baxter said, 'Thanks for coming, Dad . . . '

Mr. Baxter said, 'It's all right, son. And

don't worry much about what she said. She's overwrought, and — '

'Horace! Are you coming?' snorted Mrs. Baxter.

'Yes, m'dear.'

With a final despairing shrug of his shoulders to Eric, he left the cell.

Prenderby watched them go down the passage, then went in. He said, 'Hello, Baxter.'

'Mr. Prenderby! I'm jolly glad you came, sir. I've been feeling damned awful — '

Prenderby said, 'Buck up. All is not yet lost. Your mother was just letting off steam.'

'Oh, I don't care a hell for her. Dad isn't bad, but he allows her to rule him. It isn't *that* I'm worried about. But I do want to see the *real* murderer caught. Not — not for myself so much, as because of — of what he made Marjorie suffer. You understand, sir?'

Prenderby took his hand. He said, 'Here's my hand on it. I'll do all I can. I have a hunch that may turn out to be right. Keep your fingers crossed, and trust to luck. Now, I have to go away to see your folks back to the station. Goodbye for the moment, Baxter . . . But don't give up hope.'

He nodded. Prenderby, leaving Baxter a little more cheerful, went along the passage. The Inspector nodded to him, and went to close the cell door.

In a few more minutes the party — or, as Prenderby put to himself, 'the cortege' — was underway . . .

20

Prenderby Has an Accurate Hunch!

'Oh, ye of little sense,' breathed Prenderby, and hurried his steps to separate the two fighting Fourth Form boys at the side of North House.

'Now,' said Prenderby, holding them apart and at arms' length, 'what's the reason for this miniature riot?'

Carvel, a shock-haired young rascal with an infinite capacity for hero-worship, said:

'It's this toad Berry, sir. He was calling Baxter all kinds of names. He thinks Baxter killed that girl.'

Berry said, 'I'm entitled to an opinion, aren't I?'

' "Am I not" is the phrase,' Prenderby murmured.

'Well, sir,' said Berry, appealing to the higher authority, 'am I not?'

'You are, you are.'

'And just because I expressed one, this rotter started on me. I believe I'm going to have a black eye or something — '

Prenderby sighed. 'Better go and get Matron to put something on it.'

'Yes sir.'

'And remember, there is a time and place for settling disputes. The gymnasium, to be precise.'

'Yes sir.'

'The Quadrangle was never intended as a boxing ring.'

'We were wrestling, sir.'

'Was that what it was? Hmm . . . which style, Berry?'

'Eh?' said Berry, who hadn't heard that there were several styles of wrestling.

Prenderby eyed the two offenders sternly. He said:

'If fight you must, fight in private. Or at least, make certain that you are not observed by a strolling master — we'll say no more about this. You have been warned.'

'Thank you, sir.'

Prenderby passed on his way with a dignified mien. Round the corner he paused and waited. For a few minutes there was silence. Then a yelp, and the sound of renewed scuffling.

Prenderby peered back, cautiously.

He watched for a moment, then grunted to himself:

'Hmm. No style at all. All-in.'

Then he went on his way.

Prenderby was always lenient. But lately he had been even more lenient than usual. The truth was that his mind was full of Baxter and the murders. It was a week now since Baxter had been transferred to Exeter. And no further clues had come to light. The key from the porter's ring had borne no fingerprints but those of Brooks, who had handled it.

Possibly the murderer had had sense enough to wipe the prints off, as Prenderby had feared. So there was no evidence to show that Baxter's locked-door story was correct.

The outlook was black.

One good thing had come of the ill wind. The Swill Bin — or Scarlet Rabbit — was to be closed down. Joey Lodge was to face trial for keeping a disorderly house for minors. That menace was removed from the immediate future.

But there was the problem of Baxter.

Prenderby felt the answer was to hand. Stored somewhere in his mind, if he could but find the key to unlock it. It was like a difficult jigsaw puzzle, needing but one piece to fall into its correct position to solve the whole.

The inspector was still pursuing enquiries, which had so far resulted in nothing. The majority of people took it for granted that Baxter was the guilty party.

Prenderby turned from the playing fields and into the woods. He strolled leisurely along the narrow pathway. The midday meal was over, and there was fully an hour before he need think of getting back for afternoon classes. Lately, that hour was always spent with Mary, who met him in the woods at a halfway point.

They strolled, talked, and arranged for evening meetings.

Usually their recreation at such times took the form of a stroll with each other. Tonight, Prenderby had other plans on hand.

At Brooks' suggestion, he had arranged a card game. Personally, he was not fond of bridge. But Brooks, who had previously spent his evenings with Prenderby, was feeling pretty lonely at the moment, now that the North Housemaster found his time otherwise occupied. Prenderby felt it would not injure either Mary or himself to sit in at a bridge game.

Consequently, he was on the way to make those plans finalised.

For a fourth they had roped in Mrs. Wignall, who was a keen bridge addict. It depended only upon Mary now.

He didn't anticipate any trouble on that score. Mary was quite willing to let him hold the reins.

She was waiting in the usual place. Prenderby waved as he came up, and she smiled and took his hand.

'You're late, for the first time, John,'

'Sorry, darling. Had to stop on the way and lecture a pair of young blockheads who were pummelling each other.'

She laughed. He said:

'Could have saved myself the trouble.

Moment they thought I was out of sight and sound, they recommenced their heroic battle. I didn't want to be later still, so I had to ignore them.'

Mary said, as they strolled leisurely by the pathside: 'What were they quarrelling about?'

'Baxter.'

'Oh . . . the boy who was arrested?'

Prenderby nodded, and chuckled.

'From what I hear, young Carvel's on a crusade. He doesn't believe in free opinion and free speech. He believes in Baxter; to him, it seems sacrilege that anyone couldn't do so. His idea is that he can batter his own ideas into the heads of the dissenters by sheer physical force. He's going to have a lot of scraps on his hands, I'm afraid.'

Mary said, 'You believe in Baxter, don't you?'

'Yes. I'm quite sure he's innocent of the charge.'

Mary shook her head. 'I don't like to sound unkind, and mean, but — John, it *is* possible that Baxter killed the girl. Oh, not because she was due to bear a child to him . . . I don't think that. Really, I do think he was madly in love with her. That girl was the most bewitching little minx I've ever come across. But — I am sure she didn't return Baxter's affection. She was in the game for fun and excitement. Not for love. If it hadn't been Baxter, it would have been some other poor boy.'

'And?' queried Prenderby.

'I think that possibly she may have started taunting Baxter for some reason. Exercising her power over him — he may have lost his temper and his head, and — '

She shuddered.

Prenderby said, 'But Baxter was her lover, if we can apply the term to someone so youthful. Why would he ravish her too?'

Mary shook her head. 'He may have been temporarily insane.'

'No,' said Prenderby. 'The man who's committing these crimes is insane alright, but he's responsible for Gregg's daughter's death; and, I think, for Beasly's end. I'll not believe Baxter was guilty of those two killings. No more than I'll believe he killed the girl he loved.'

She said, 'I see the Sunday newspapers got hold of the story.'

'Yes. It's practically turned Dr. Wignall's hair pure white. Reporters have been haunting the school, digging up all sorts of odd facts. They've even got wind of Gregg's wood-prowling activities.'

'He's still in hospital, isn't he?'

'He's due out in a couple of days.'

They strolled in silence for a time. At length, Mary said, 'It's getting late. How about tonight, John?'

They stopped. He said, 'Would you mind very much if we didn't have our usual walk? Brooks has been a bit put out at nights since we've been seeing each other. He suggested we play bridge tonight: you and Mrs. Wignall, and he and myself. You don't mind, do you, Mary?'

'Why, no, John.' She frowned.

Prenderby said, 'If you'd rather not . . .'

'Oh, I like bridge. It isn't that. It's just — Brooks.'

'Brooks?'

She nodded. 'I don't much like him, you know.'

Prenderby said, 'That's strange. He likes you a great deal.'

She shrugged. 'I know — he used to hang around me at the dance a lot.'

'What have you got against him? I find him a very likeable chap.'

'It isn't anything I can put my finger on. I just feel — well, that he's — strange.'

'Woman's intuition, eh?' smiled Prenderby.

'Call it that.'

Prenderby laughed, his eyes twinkling with affection for Mary.

'Possibly you sense that Brooks has more than a friendly interest in you, my dear. Maybe that's what annoys you.'

'It isn't that at all. I simply don't like him. I find him a bit creepy.'

Prenderby said, 'Then I'll call the bridge off, shall I?'

'Oh, no! Don't do that. It isn't that bad.'

Prenderby saw her almost to Munston

School, and then turned and walked back to take his class. He was thinking that if Wignall retired, he would be appointed Headmaster; and, if so, he would need a wife — like, for example, Mary.

★　★　★

'I really must be going now,' said Mrs. Wignall, smiling as she got up. 'Samuel has developed the habit of retiring early lately — and I like to see his bed turned down for him myself. Thank you, Mr. Prenderby — and you, Miss Nightingale, and Brooks. It really has been quite an absorbing game.'

She smiled at them again, and took her departure.

Brooks yawned, and smiled at Prenderby and Mary.

'I suppose I'd better crawl to my little nest and leave the two lovebirds alone, eh?'

Prenderby said, 'Don't be silly, old man — '

Brooks grinned. 'I don't want to intrude. Found out any more about the murders, Prenderby? Inspector any further forward?'

Prenderby shook his head. 'He isn't. Really, the whole thing hinges on one point, if we're to believe Baxter innocent — the key. The porter certified nobody could have replaced it the morning following the murder — and yet someone must have done.'

Brooks chuckled: 'Keys are funny things. I mean, because a certain key fits a door, you can't say that no *other* key would have sufficed.'

Mary said, 'You mean one might have been made specifically for the purpose?'

Prenderby said, 'No, that isn't possible. How did the killer know Baxter had an appointment in the woods with the girl? Clearly, only by finding the note Baxter dropped. In that case he wouldn't have had time to have had a key made.'

Brooks interjected: 'But, at the same time, how do you know it was the killer who locked Baxter in? Might have been a joke.'

'If we believe Baxter innocent, we can take it for granted that the whole events of the murder and the locked door sprang from that note being found. Probably Baxter was seen to drop it. After having digested the contents, the murderer acted accordingly. And we do know the note was found at the scene of the crime, which proves the killer had possession of it, and most likely dropped it purposely.'

'It all comes back to the key again,' said Brooks. 'But what I mean, when I say another key could have been used, was that the murderer might have found one of his own keys fitted the lock. It isn't unusual, you know. When I was at Oxford, we had study keys, and mine fitted at least two other studies for which it was not intended. Then again, when I was on holiday in Brighton last vac., my Uncle had a rather exquisite desk, the drawer of which he'd never been able to unlock, owing to losing the key. He'd tried all kinds of things, outside of having a key made. In the end, he had one made — and then, to his annoyance, found that the key to his writing-case would have done the trick just as well!'

He stopped talking, for Prenderby was

staring at him fixedly.

'Anything wrong, old man?'

'Eh? No — no, not at all.'

Mary said, significantly: 'I must be going, John.'

'Yes, dear,' said Prenderby. He made no effort to move.

Brooks stood up. 'Well, I'll push off — '

'No, hang on a moment, Brooks. I'd like to speak to you after Mary's gone.'

Brooks stared. 'Aren't you seeing Mary home?'

'Oh — oh no. Not tonight. Well, you'll be all right, won't you Mary? I mean, it's quite moonlit out.'

Mary flushed, bit her lip.

'You mean — ? Oh, yes, I'll be all right. I can cut across the woods — quicker that way.'

Brooks looked at Prenderby curiously. 'She can't cross the woods alone, old man. It isn't safe.'

Prenderby said woodenly: 'I'm sure she'll be all right. I'm a bit fagged, if you must have the truth, and I have some papers to check. Good night, Mary.'

She said, stiffly, 'Good night, John.'

He didn't even mention meeting the next day.

Brooks said quickly: 'Look here, I'll see you home if Pren's tired — '

'No, Brooks. I want to speak to you. It's quite important.'

Mary added: 'I'll be quite safe, I'm sure.'

Actually, she wasn't too sure. She almost hoped that she *would* run into trouble in the woods — then he'd be sorry he'd allowed her to leave like that. What on earth was wrong with him?

Prenderby saw her into the passage. He kissed her quickly, said, 'You'll be safe, my dear. I'm sorry about this, but I have a hunch — and I want to try it out *now*. As for the killer — you won't meet him, Mary — I can vouch for *that*!'

She said, 'I trust you, darling. I know it must be important, whatever it is. Good night, John.'

'See you tomorrow, Mary. Same place and time.'

She saw herself out into the dark Quad, and hurried round towards the playing fields and the woods.

Prenderby turned back into the study. Brooks was sitting in a straight chair near the fire. He looked at Prenderby curiously.

'Must be something important, old man?'

'It is. Very.'

Brooks said, 'Really? What is it? Want to ask me to be your best man?' He grinned.

Prenderby said, 'No — nothing of that nature.'

'She's a damned sweet girl, that one. Don't know how you could let her hare off alone and risk meeting the murderer.'

'She won't meet the murderer.'

Said Brooks, curiously: 'She won't? What makes you so sure?'

'Because,' said Prenderby grimly, 'the murderer is *right here in this study*!'

Brooks' face was a picture.

For several seconds neither Prenderby nor Brooks spoke. The younger man seemed stunned by the revelation. His eyes wandered round the study, as if he expected to see someone hiding behind the curtains.

Finally he laughed, uneasily:

'Don't talk rot, Prenderby.'

'I'm quite serious. The murderer is here.'

Brooks flushed. He said:

'If you're — good God! Prenderby — you — you aren't confessing, are you? Man — '

'You know better than that, Brooks. I'm not confessing — I'm hoping you will!'

Brooks' eyes began to show a trace of panic.

'What the devil do you mean? You don't think I — you can't think I'm the man.'

Prenderby spoke quietly.

'Yes, I mean that I think you are the man. That's why I let Mary go home alone. As long as you're here with me, she won't be in any danger,'

Brooks' tone was sullen. He said:

'You're mad, Prenderby. You'd better explain yourself.'

'I will. For days now, I've had the feeling that the elusive clue was right at my fingertips. Tonight, you helped me to find it. I didn't realise until then . . . Brooks, tonight you mentioned *Oxford* and *Brighton*, in conjunction with the matter of the keys we'd been discussing. And it suddenly struck me that at both those places similar murders to those committed here have taken place, and the murderers have not been caught. At Oxford, during the time you were there, two women were killed. Then Gregg's girl here at Munston. And — the impressive link — a girl was killed in like manner on the beach at *Brighton* — at roughly the same time that *you* were visiting your uncle during the holidays!'

Brooks laughed — uneasily. 'That doesn't prove anything. Just coincidence.'

'No — wait — having seen that far, I began to see the rest. The problem of Baxter's defence hinged on whether anyone had taken that particular master key from the porter's lodge. The knotty point was how could they have restored it to the ring before you went along to bring it for the Inspector. And the answer, Brooks, is that it *wasn't* restored to the ring until you had the ring in your possession! You hooked it back when you were returning to the study — and fooled everyone. It didn't even matter that your fingerprints were on it, then. It was *you* who found the note Baxter had dropped — you who planned how you would attack and kill the girl — you who locked poor Baxter in his study . . . '

Brooks was half out of his seat. His facial muscles were working, his eyes were peculiar in their expression. 'You're a liar, Prenderby!' he shouted.

'I'm not. First Oxford — then Munston — and Brighton. You killed women at all these places. Gregg's daughter: first to be attacked here — shortly after *you* came to the school. Only then did the murders here start. And you had the opportunity to know she was going through the woods alone . . . Beasly, too. God knows why, but I'm convinced you killed *him*. You said you were up in the boxroom to throw away an old bat — my guess is, you had an arrangement to meet Beasly there. Why? Was he extorting all that money from *you*, as well as Chester? I remember you were always borrowing last term. Always hard-up. And Beasly told his bookie that he'd have the money

355

before he left. A large sum — did he plan to get it from you? Did he fail — because you had decided to shut his mouth forever?'

Brooks' lips were working. His eyes were flaring wildly at the accusing figure of Prenderby.

Prenderby said: 'It *was* you, Brooks!'

Brooks laughed — an unbalanced laugh.

'You're smart, Prenderby. I couldn't stand up to an investigation. Yes — it was me! *Me!* I was clever, too.'

Prenderby reached for the phone. Brooks slumped into his chair, the wildness leaving his face. In a subdued voice he said:

'Wait — don't call anyone yet. Not yet — let me get it off my conscience. Let me tell you the whole sorry damned tale! Hear me out, Prenderby — it can't harm you.'

Prenderby hesitated. Then he said, 'Right.'

But he stayed close to the telephone. Watchful.

Brooks wrung his hands together. He

looked down at the floor.

'I've been so damned — miserable, Prenderby. God knows how I've kept up the act. Trying to look cheerful . . . you see, I can't help myself. I don't actually black out when I have my attacks, but I can't hold myself back. I've always been a pretty shy sort of chap where women are concerned. And they always seemed to fight shy of me. Perhaps — perhaps it was because that extra sense they like to call their intuition kind of gave them an inkling of — what was under the surface in me.'

Prenderby remembered what Mary had said. 'Go on, Brooks.'

Brooks muttered, 'The thing first started a few weeks after I'd recovered from a nervous breakdown at Oxford, brought on by overwork. It was a local barmaid — I waited for her in a side lane, after the pub had closed, and — it happened. I didn't mean to — to kill her. Just wanted her to be nice to me. I — I knew that she was loose, had had to do with a lot of the other chaps. But she wouldn't wear me. She made that clear.

Laughed in my face — scoffed at me. Before I knew where I was, I'd struck her, when her cries alarmed me. I — went mad. I — strangled her, to keep her quiet. Soon she lay still. I hadn't meant to kill her altogether. But I was afraid now. She would name me if she recovered. To make sure the job was properly done, I battered her head in.'

His brow was dewed with great, glistening drops of perspiration. He continued, 'After that there was another — just before I left Oxford. I kept hoping I'd conquer my horrible lust. For that first killing had set a train in motion. I had experienced a thrill when I felt her soft throat under my fingers — her writhing, kicking body gradually growing still. And later, when I'd felt her flesh and bone pulp to mush under the end of a heavy, fallen log I'd used to batter her head in. I wanted to experience the same sensations again . . .

'I arrived here. And on my seventh night, heard that Gregg's daughter's escort had injured himself and that she would be walking through the woods alone. There'd never been a murder here — no one expected there would be any danger for her. Nor was there, until I came.

'I followed her — attacked her. She recognised me, and I had to kill her. I'd have killed her anyhow. The lust for that was strong in me.

'God, Prenderby, how I hated myself!

'But what was worse was that there was someone else in the woods that night. Someone who — watched us!

'He had been there with a village wench. Or so he told me later. He was a filthy little swine. I hated him. And I hated him more so when he began to blackmail me on pain of exposing my secret!

'Yes, that was *Beasly*. A regular little blackmailer. He was blackmailing Chester — perhaps others, too. He had me at my wits' ends with his demands. All my salary went to him. And even so, he gambled away more than he had. He owed his bookie money. He came to me the night before term-end, wanting fifty quid. He didn't care where it came from, he had to have it.

'I said I hadn't that much, and he advised me to get it quickly. It was urgent, he told me. I said I'd do what I could, and we arranged to meet where we wouldn't be seen — in the boxroom, shortly before he was due to leave. I was there at the appointed time. He wasn't. Later, it turned out you'd sent for him to jaw him about the notebook of his you'd found. I grew tired of waiting, and went downstairs. I passed Chester as he was going up. And immediately the idea of ridding myself of Beasly was simplified. Chester could be the scapegoat!

'I wasted no time. Knowing Chester was away from his study, I hurried over there. I took his lighter, and his handkerchief. Those were the most obvious items, and items he might not miss, it being so close to term-end. Then I hurried back again. I took care that I was not seen. I hung round the passages until Chester had got clear. I saw Beasly rush from his study and go to the boxroom. Then I went after him.

'Five minutes later he was dead, and I

had a hectic rush to catch my train. When I joined you in that compartment, I'd actually come fresh from my crime. It was an awful strain to keep up a jolly front.'

Brooks paused again, and buried his head in his hands.

'I found the note to Baxter — and everything afterwards was as you said. I took the key whilst the porter was out — not the afternoon before, as he had suggested it might have been. It was actually late at night, on my way back from the dance. My plan was formed beforehand. I knocked at his door, and asked him to help me. I told him I suspected some of the North House boys of breaking bounds. Said they were juniors, and I'd seen them coming along the road behind me.

'I waited at the gates, and sent him round to the broken part of the wall to — as I told him — stop them coming in there. He went. I slipped into the lodge and took the master key. I didn't worry about getting it back then. That would come later.

'When he came back, I said I'd caught

the juniors, taken their names, and would report them to you. He didn't suspect I'd purloined the key!

'Later, I locked Baxter in, and kept the appointment myself. That fool Gregg came pottering along — I knocked him out and left him. I might have finished him off, but the girl happened to arrive just at that moment . . . the rest, you can guess.'

Brooks stopped talking. He raised a drawn face to Prenderby.

He said, 'Prenderby — do me one favour?'

21

In This Proud Castle

Prenderby had not spoken during the recital of Brooks' vicious narrative. Now he said, his hand halfway towards the phone:

'What is it?'

'Let me telephone the police *myself* — give myself up.'

'I doubt if it would do any good.'

'It may. Anyhow, when the trial comes up, it would sound better if the jury were told I'd telephoned the police myself.'

Prenderby said, 'All right, Brooks. I don't want any credit in this thing.'

Brooks said, 'I must admit I owe you a few grudges, Prenderby. First *Mary* — now *this* . . . ' He sighed.

Prenderby was taking no chances. He kept his hand resting on a metal ashtray as Brooks came over.

But Brooks seemed completely subdued. He said, 'What's the number?'

'Branshoot 1020.'

Brooks nodded, and reached for the cradled receiver.

Prenderby could never have suspected it. It hadn't struck him that the phone would be an ideal weapon, and one Brooks could secure without attracting suspicion.

Brooks picked the phone up by the earpiece. And unexpectedly swung the slack of the wire free, brought the phone back and drove it forward viciously, with tremendous force, at Prenderby's head.

The narrow lip of the mouthpiece cracked sharply against the North Housemaster's forehead, just above the bridge of his nose.

And whilst he was staggering, dazedly, Brooks dealt a second, and a third, blow.

Prenderby went down — and, simultaneously, there was a knock at the door.

Brooks turned, sprinted for the window. He went right through, bursting the two sides open, and shattering the glass.

The study door opened, and Wignall came in.

'Prenderby — the hospital have telephoned to say that Gregg has sneaked out, and has probably made for the woods again. He has to be found — Good God! What — what is all *this*?'

Prenderby crawled to his knees. His head was singing, but he forced himself to conquer the nausea that swept over him in waves.

He gasped: 'Brooks — no time to explain now, but — he's the killer. Knocked me out with — phone. I — think he'll head for — the woods. Mary — Mary Nightingale is out there. He — he's insane. Must know the game's up, and may try to — hurt her, to score off — me.'

Wignall said, 'Good Heavens! *Gregg* is out there, too.'

Prenderby shook his head to clear it, and said, 'Phone the police and tell them what's happened. I'm going — '

He didn't wait for any further useless conversation. He went — taking the same shortcut as Brooks, through the window.

Then he was running across the Quad, to the playing fields and over them, panting and gasping, still dizzy from the blows he'd received, but desperate at the idea of Mary being in danger.

He ran like a man possessed. He prayed that Mary would have reached Munston, but knew that it was impossible. A girl had to go slowly through the woods at night. There were far too many ruts to catch high heels; the route was tortuous and twisting.

No — if Brooks meant to go after her, and stuck to the path, with a turn of speed he must surely catch her up long before she reached safety.

Prenderby raced on. He was no longer young, though he was in good shape. But even so, such a run at his age was no light matter.

He could have fallen exhausted to the ground many times, but he kept going.

Through the darkest part of the path — and suddenly he crashed into another running figure, and both went down.

Prenderby was alert at once — and then:

'*Mary!* Thank God — '

She sobbed: 'John — hurry — hurry — '

She was almost too winded to speak. Her dress had been torn completely from her, and her underthings had suffered in her wild flight through the woods. She was dishevelled and dirty.

She panted: 'It's Brooks — *Brooks!* He attacked me — overtook me on the path. John — he'd have killed me I'm sure, but — *Gregg* burst out of the trees. Heaven only knows where he came from . . . he threw himself on Brooks — I was in such a panic that I came away and left them struggling, I was running for help. Oh, John, hurry. He'll kill poor Gregg. He's mad!'

Prenderby was up and running again, along the path towards the Scarlet Rabbit.

Gregg, at the hands of that madman! And really still a hospital case!

Prenderby burst from the turn, and came to a scene of unbelievable bedlam. Two figures on the path ahead — one fallen on the path and writhing wildly, screaming — the second armed with what appeared to be a thick tree branch, shrieking imprecations at the fallen one, and battering fiercely at the other man's head and shoulders with the crude weapon.

Prenderby put on speed.

He reached the upright figure — caught its arm, and wrenched the branch free. Threw it aside. The figure calmed. A pair of wild eyes turned towards him, gradually glazing as the madness left them.

Prenderby shuddered, and glanced down at the battered face and head of the man lying on the path. No doubt but that he was dead now! Pulped unmercifully.

The glazed eyes looked at Prenderby, and a strangely awed voice said, 'Have I killed him?'

Prenderby said, 'Yes.'

'I said I would. I knew the woods would give him up sooner or later. I knew it.'

Prenderby said, gently: 'It was lucky for Mary that you happened along. Come on, Gregg, old man. It's all over.'

Gregg, leaning on Prenderby's arm, allowed himself to be led away.

The shapeless, faceless thing that had been Brooks lay, a bloody, pulped mess, on the back path behind the Scarlet Rabbit.

★ ★ ★

Dr. Wignall took Prenderby's hand, and shook it firmly.

'So it's goodbye, Prenderby,' he smiled. 'The end of another eventful term — and next term, one of the absent faces will be my own . . . '

'Are you really content to retire, sir?'

'I am. This term has been too much for me, and my wife. I leave the school in more capable hands — young blood, Prenderby, eh? You'll tide the old place over.'

Prenderby said, 'I can't thank you enough for your words of recommendation to the Governors, sir.'

'Don't try. You're the obvious man for the job, Prenderby. I wish you jolly good luck, and if at any time I can be of assistance, don't hesitate to let me know.'

'Thank you.'

'And I also wish you every joy in your marriage,' said Dr. Wignall, with a very unscholarly wink. 'She's a pretty bit of fluff, Prenderby. Very pretty. But sensible. I'm sure she'll fill my wife's place admirably — er — without, of course, displacing quite so much *air*!'

He chuckled. 'When are you being married Prenderby? During the break?'

'That's right, sir. So we'll be able to take over as man and wife in the new term.'

'Headmaster and wife,' corrected Dr. Wignall. He sighed. 'I can remember when I was your age — younger, even — taking over here. I had some very startling ideas then, Prenderby.'

'Really, sir?'

Wignall eyed him closely. 'Indeed I did. I actually had some fantastic notion about a Free School — letting scholars have their own ways to develop their latent personalities.'

'Good God!' said Prenderby.

'You wouldn't have suspected, eh?

Because I'm such a typical old diehard headmaster. But I wasn't once — and Prenderby — you've never actually spoken forthrightly to me on the subject, but I have a feeling that *you* believe in a new order of public schools?'

Prenderby said, 'Yes, sir. There are some reforms I'd like to see — '

Wignall shook his head.

'You try to move too fast, and you'll trip yourself up. Remember that you have a wife to think of now, and possibly children. You can't risk this job by putting your ideas into practise. You'll never find a post as good — isn't that right? You have to abandon your idealism — marriage almost always kills that anyway. In more ways than one, eh? I know it's hard to feel you'll never have that free hand you've wanted. I always felt the same. And yet, I had to curb my ideas to be sure of security for my family. Unfortunately, only a wife in my case — but you'll have children, no doubt?'

Prenderby looked a little glum. He knew Wignall was right. He had responsibilities now. He could not risk being dismissed for the sake of trying out his theories. This was a public school, not a private one. If he had intended to remain single . . . but Mary was worth it, and more.

'You're right, Doctor. I'll behave.'

'You need not abandon your principles altogether. But slowly, my boy. Take your time. In time, you can carry my work several steps further — '

Prenderby said, 'Your work?'

Wignall's eyes twinkled. He chuckled. 'Who do you imagine abolished that outdated practice of fagging at St. Mark's? I did. Who fought for the abolition of flogging? Same again. Only two reforms — but a start. A step in the direction of my ultimate goal. And now — you can work on removing the power of the seniors to cane junior boys. Take the ashplant away from prefects. Let that be your slogan, Prenderby. I fear the prefects are apt to abuse the powers they wield. *And* the ashplants, *and* the recipients thereof.'

He smiled, and held out his hand. 'Goodbye, my dear chap! And good luck!'

Prenderby stood by the gates. Mary was beside him. The last coachload of exuberant juniors was rolling from the Quad. Eager hands waved.

'Bye, sir.'

'Have a nice time.'

Prenderby waved back. 'I will.'

Pritchet, at the rear of the coach, turned to a friend and said:

'I *bet* he will with a piece of stuff like Mary. I could fancy it myself.'

Prenderby, eyeing Pritchet's bus-borne back, murmured: 'I can guess what that young son of Satan was saying!'

Mary said, 'What, darling?'

'Eh? Oh, nothing, dear. Nothing.'

Gregg turned out of School House and proceeded towards the gates, carrying a suitcase. 'Just off, Prenderby,' he smiled. 'Expect we'll be calling you 'Sir' next term.'

Prenderby said, 'Not a bit of it. That can be my first reform. The name remains, as always, Prenderby. And I'll expect you to treat me no differently.'

Gregg grinned, shook hands; and, after murmuring something about there being nothing like a nice, brisk walk, strode off on foot towards Munston.

Mary said, 'Hasn't he improved wonderfully since that awful business was cleared up?'

'He certainly has. Quite his old jovial self these days.'

'He is.'

After a few moments, she said:

'How about Baxter? The last I heard of him, after he was expelled, was that his mother had forbidden him the house because of his disgraceful conduct.'

Prenderby said, 'Strangely enough, I had a letter from him just yesterday. It seems that Marjorie's parents got in touch with him, and offered him a decent job.'

'*Marjorie's parents?*' she gasped. 'But surely they'd have a down on him?'

'It doesn't seem that way. Some people can understand better than others. Perhaps Marjorie's folks know how Baxter feels — '

They turned, and walked towards the

house. Mary said: 'If I know your views, there'll be some changes made here next term.'

Prenderby shook his head slowly, and smiled. He said:

'No, Mary. I think not.'

She was surprised. 'But I thought — '

'That you'd see your prospective husband on a grand crusade?'

'Yes.' She smiled.

Prenderby put his arm round her. He murmured: 'I've had a change of mind, Mary. Changes there will be — but very gradual — ' He broke off to nod to a passing Fifth Former, and to say:

'You won't be with us next term, eh, Haines? Well, be sure to drop me a line, my boy.'

'I will, sir,' said Haines, without the slightest intention in the world of doing so.

'Goodbye,' said Prenderby, and added, *sotto voce*: 'I bet he will.'

He looked at Mary. 'Where was I?'

'In the middle of a gradual change.'

'Oh yes,' he said, gazing ahead at the grey stones of the School and North

Houses, and the ugly red brick of their intrusive companion house. 'Changes will be gradual — very gradual. For a while, life will go on as it always has in this proud castle!'

THE END